Jason and the Argonauts: A Retelling in Prose of Apollonius of Rhodes' Argonautica

David Bruce

Published by David Bruce, 2022.

This is a work of fiction. Similarities to real people, places, or events are entirely coincidental.

JASON AND THE ARGONAUTS: A RETELLING IN PROSE OF APOLLONIUS OF RHODES' ARGONAUTICA

First edition. July 6, 2022.

Copyright © 2022 David Bruce.

ISBN: 979-8201905057

Written by David Bruce.

Table of Contents

Dedication

Dedicated to Carl Eugene Bruce and Josephine Saturday Bruce

My father, Carl Eugene Bruce, died on 24 October 2013. He used to work for Ohio Power, and at one time, his job was to shut off the electricity of people who had not paid their bills. He sometimes would find a home with an impoverished mother and some children. Instead of shutting off their electricity, he would tell the mother that she needed to pay her bill or soon her electricity would be shut off. He would write on a form that no one was home when he stopped by because if no one was home he did not have to shut off their electricity.

The best good deed that anyone ever did for my father occurred after a storm that knocked down many power lines. He and other linemen worked long hours and got wet and cold. Their feet were freezing because water got into their boots and soaked their socks. Fortunately, a kind woman gave my father and the other linemen dry socks to wear.

My mother, Josephine Saturday Bruce, died on 14 June 2003. She used to work at a store that sold clothing. One day, an impoverished mother with a baby clothed in rags walked into the store and started shoplifting in an interesting way: The mother took the rags off her baby and dressed the infant in new clothing. My mother knew that this mother could not afford to buy the clothing, but she helped the mother dress her baby and then she watched as the mother walked out of the store without paying.

***

The doing of good deeds is important. As a free person, you can choose to live your life as a good person or as a bad person. To be a good person, do good deeds. To be a bad person, do bad deeds. If you do good deeds, you will become good. If you do bad deeds, you will become bad. To become the person you want to be, act as if you already are that kind of person. Each of us chooses what kind of person we will become. To become a good person, do the things a good person does. To become a bad person, do the things a bad person does. The opportunity to take action to become the kind of person you want to be is yours.

Human beings have free will. According to the Babylonian Niddah 16b, whenever a baby is to be conceived, the Lailah (angel in charge of contraception) takes the drop of semen that will result in the conception and asks God, "Sovereign of the Universe, what is going to be the fate of this drop? Will it develop into a robust or into a weak person? An intelligent or a stupid person? A wealthy or a poor person?" The Lailah asks all these questions, but it does not ask, "Will it develop into a righteous or a wicked person?" The answer to that question lies in the decisions to be freely made by the human being that is the result of the conception.

A Buddhist monk visiting a class wrote this on the chalkboard: "EVERYONE WANTS TO SAVE THE WORLD, BUT NO ONE WANTS TO HELP MOM DO THE DISHES." The students laughed, but the monk then said, "Statistically, it's highly unlikely that any of you will ever have the opportunity to run into a burning orphanage and rescue an infant. But, in the smallest gesture of kindness — a warm smile, holding the door for the person behind you, shoveling the driveway of the elderly person next door — you have committed an act of immeasurable profundity, because to each of us, our life is our universe."

In her book titled *I Have Chosen to Stay and Fight*, comedian Margaret Cho writes, "I believe that we get complimentary snack-size portions of the afterlife, and we all receive them in a different way." For Ms. Cho, many of her snack-size portions of the afterlife come in hip hop music. Other people get different snack-size portions of the afterlife, and we all must be on the lookout for them when they come our way. And perhaps doing good deeds and experiencing good deeds are snack-size portions of the afterlife.

The Zen master Gisan was taking a bath. The water was too hot, so he asked a student to add some cold water to the bath. The student brought a bucket of cold water, added some cold water to the bath, and then threw the rest of the water on a rocky path. Gisan scolded the student: "Everything can be used. Why did you waste the rest of the water by pouring it on the path? There are some plants nearby which could have used the water. What right do you have to waste even a drop of water?" The student became enlightened and changed his name to Tekisui, which means "Drop of Water."

Cover Photograph for *Jason and the Argonauts*:
Institutnationalhistoiredelart
http://tinyurl.com/hqjhbsl
https://www.flickr.com/photos/73632227@N02/
https://creativecommons.org/licenses/by/2.0/

***

Educate Yourself
Read Like A Wolf Eats
Be Excellent to Each Other
Books Then, Books Now, Books Forever

***

In this retelling, as in all my retellings, I have tried to make the work of literature accessible to modern readers who may lack the knowledge about mythology, religion, and history that the literary work's contemporary audience had.

Do you know a language other than English? If you do, I give you permission to translate this book, copyright your translation, publish or self-publish it, and keep all the royalties for yourself. (Do give me credit, of course, for the original retelling.)

I would like to see my retellings of classic literature used in schools, so I give permission to the country of Finland (and all other countries) to give copies of any or all of my retellings to all students forever. I also give permission to the state of Texas (and all other states) to give copies of any or all of my retellings to all students forever. I also give permission to all teachers to give copies of any or all of my retellings to all students forever. Of course, libraries are welcome to use my eBooks for free.

Teachers need not actually teach my retellings. Teachers are welcome to give students copies of my eBooks as background material. For example, if they are teaching Homer's *Iliad* and *Odyssey*, teachers are welcome to give students copies of my *Virgil's* Aeneid: *A Retelling in Prose* and tell them, "Here's another ancient epic you may want to read in your spare time."

Preface

The heroes of the Trojan War — Achilles, Hector, Odysseus, Agamemnon, etc. — are well known. However, the generation before the heroes of the Trojan War also had its heroes. Many of these heroes voyaged on the ship *Argo* with Jason in his quest to acquire the Golden Fleece. Some of the Argonauts — the sailors of the ship named the *Argo* — were the fathers of some of the Trojan War heroes: Peleus was the father of Achilles, Telamon was the father of Great Ajax, Oileus was the father of Little Ajax, and Menoetius was the father of Patroclus. In addition, the Argonauts included the twins Polydeuces and Castor, the brothers of Helen of Troy.

The Golden Fleece

The ram with the Golden Fleece rescued a child: Phrixus, the son of Athamas and Nephele in southeastern Greece. Athamas had married Nephele, and she bore him two children: a son named Phrixus and a daughter named Helle. But Athamas ceased to love Nephele, and he married Ino. Nephele left. Ino was a cruel stepmother to Phrixus and Helle, and she plotted against them and wanted them to die. Nephele returned to rescue her children. She sent them a winged ram whose fleece was made of gold. Phrixus and Helle climbed on top of the ram, which flew them over the sea. Unfortunately, Helle fell off the ram into the sea and drowned; thereafter, that sea was called the Hellespont in honor of her. The ram carried Phrixus from Greece to Colchis on the eastern shore of the Black Sea. Phrixus lived there in the palace of King Aeetes, and he sacrificed the ram to the sea-god Poseidon. He skinned the ram and hung its Golden Fleece on a tree where a huge snake guarded it. This is the Golden Fleece that Jason and the heroes who sailed with him sought.

Jason's Early Years

Jason's father was named Aeson, and his mother was named Alcimede. Aeson was the rightful ruler of Thessaly, but Pelias, his half-brother, overthrew him and assumed the throne, which was in Iolcus, for himself. Pelias wanted to kill all of Aeson's children, but Alcimede was able to save Jason's life when he was born. She tricked Pelias into thinking that Jason was stillborn by having the women who served her pretend to mourn Jason. She sent Jason to the wise Centaur Chiron to raise to adulthood.

Jason Goes to Iolcus

Hera, the wife of Zeus, king of gods and men, hated Pelias, who had killed his stepmother, Sidero, who had mistreated his mother, Tyro. He killed his stepmother on an altar dedicated to Hera, which is sacrilegious. Because of Pelias' act of impiety, Hera hated him. In return, Pelias did not worship Hera. Because of her hatred of Pelias, Hera became Jason's patron goddess. She knew that one day Jason would marry Medea, who would cause the death of Pelias. When Jason came of age, he decided to see Pelias, who had been warned by an oracle to beware of a man wearing one sandal. Jason wanted to regain the throne for his father, who still lived. Jason came to a stream, where he saw an old woman who wanted to cross the water. The old woman was Hera in disguise; she wanted to see what kind of man Jason was. Was Jason a good man who would help an old woman? Or was Jason a bad man who would refuse to help an old woman? Jason carried her on his back across the water, and Hera knew that Jason deserved her help. As Jason crossed the water, he lost one sandal. Hera told Jason to go to the city of Iolcus in Thessaly and see Pelias, and she told him that he — Jason — would have her help.

When Jason arrived in Iolcus, Pelias saw that he was wearing one sandal. Pelias would have liked to have Jason killed immediately, but he did not want to incite the people of Iolcus to rebel against him. Jason told Pelias that he wanted him to give the throne to Aeson, Jason's father. Pelias said that both he and Aeson were old and tired, but that Jason was young and vigorous, and so Jason should be the King of Thessaly — if he could prove himself worthy. Pelias also said that an exploit that would prove that Jason was worthy of being King of Thessaly would be for Jason to acquire the Golden Fleece in Colchis on the eastern shore of the Black Sea. Privately, Pelias believed and hoped that Jason would die in the attempt to acquire the Golden Fleece.

Jason accepted the challenge. He decided to build a ship, assemble a group of heroes, and sail away in the quest to acquire the Golden Fleece.

Chapter 1: The Argo Sets Sail

King Pelias of Thessaly sent Jason and the Argonauts on the quest to acquire the Golden Fleece. Through an oracle, he had learned that a man wearing one sandal would cause his death. Soon, a man arrived at his court wearing one sandal. That man was Jason, who had lost his sandal while helping an old woman cross a flooded river. Jason had arrived on a feast day — a day on which Pelias gave a feast in honor of his father, the sea-god Poseidon, and all other gods and goddesses, except for Hera, whom he would not worship. (Pelias' stepmother had mistreated his mother, so when he became an adult, he killed his stepmother, who had fled into a temple dedicated to Hera. This was a sacrilege, and Hera ever afterward hated him.)

Pelias saw the man with one sandal and immediately decided to send him on a dangerous quest — a quest on which the man with one sandal would perish either on land or at sea.

Quickly, the quest was arranged, and a shipwright named Argus built the *Argo*, the ship on which the heroes would journey to Colchis on the eastern shore of the Black Sea, the city where the Golden Fleece was located. In building the *Argo*, Argus had the help of the goddess Athena, who instructed him to use a beam from the palace as the prow of the ship. The beam came from a tree that had grown in Dodona, where a shrine was dedicated to Zeus, king of gods and men.

Heroes heard of the quest, and they came to Iolcus to serve as the crew of the *Argo* and to gain glory and fame.

Orpheus

Orpheus came to join the quest. His mother was the goddess Calliope, the muse of epic poetry. His father was a mortal: Oeagrus of Thrace. Orpheus was a singer of songs, and his skill was so great that his songs could enchant and move boulders and streams. On the coast of Thrace are wild oaks that heard his songs and moved by themselves like ranks of soldiers from high on a mountain down to the coast. Such was the skill of Orpheus with lyre and voice. The Centaur Chiron recommended that Jason make Orpheus a member of his crew, and Jason did.

Later, after the quest, Orpheus would mourn the death of Eurydice, his wife, so much that he would go to the Land of the Dead in an attempt to bring her back to the Land of the Living. He appeared before Hades, the ruler of the Land of the Dead, and Persephone, Hades' queen, and he played sad music for them. Hades agreed to let Eurydice return to the Land of the Living — on one condition: Orpheus had to walk in front of her and not look at her until both he and his wife were in the Land of the Living. Orpheus led her up out of the Land of the Dead, but he was so eager to see her again that as soon as he stepped into the Land of the Living he turned around and looked at her. Unfortunately, Eurydice was still one step away from the Land of the Living. She said to him, "Farewell" — and disappeared.

Asterion

Asterion, the son of Cometes, joined the crew of the *Argo*.

Polyphemus

Polyphemus lived in the city of Larissa in Thrace, but when he was young, he had fought the wild Centaurs when they got drunk at the wedding of Pirithous to Hippodamia in the land of the Lapiths. The Centaurs were unused to drinking wine, and the wine made them drunk and reckless. The Centaur Eurytion attempted to rape Hippodamia, and the Lapiths, assisted by Theseus, King of Athens, fought the Centaurs and defeated them. This battle between the Lapiths and the Centaurs became known as the Centauromachy. Now Polyphemus was a much older man, yet he still had the fighting spirit of a young man.

Iphiclus

Iphiclus, one of Jason's uncles, joined the quest. His sister was Alcimede, the wife of Aeson, and because of the ties of kinship, he would not be left behind.

Admetus

Admetus, the King of Pherae, was a rich man, and his country had many sheep. Still, he sought adventure, and he did not want to stay in his town beneath the peak of Mount Chalcodon. Apollo served King Admetes for one year as a punishment for killing the Cyclopes who forged thunderbolts for Jupiter. He did this for revenge after Jupiter had killed Apollo's son Asclepius because Asclepius was able to raise the dead, something which went against fate. King Admetes treated Apollo well, and Apollo later helped King Admetus marry Alcestis. In one version of the myth, Jupiter resurrected the Cyclopes and Asclepius.

Erytus, Echion, and Aethalides

At this time, gods still slept with mortals, and Erytus and Echion were the sons of Hermes, the messenger god whose winged feet made him swift. A kinsman named Aethalides came with them to join the quest. Aethalides was also a son of Hermes, who had given him an infallible memory.

Coronus

Coronus, the son of Caeneus, joined the quest. He was a brave man, and his father was as brave or braver. When the Lapiths fought the Centaurs, Caeneus fought bravely and pushed the Centaurs back, but they regrouped and attacked him. They were unable to kill him because he was invulnerable, but they defeated him by burying him alive under an immense pile of the trunks of pine trees.

Mopsus

Mopsus brought the prophetic art to the crew of the *Argo*. Apollo, the god of prophecy, had himself trained him in the arts of divination. Mopsus surpassed all other mortals in interpreting the flight of birds.

Eurydamas

Eurydamas, who lived in Thessaly, also joined the quest.

Menoetius

The man named Actor sent Menoetius, his son, to join the quest. Menoetius was the father of Patroclus, who would become Achilles' best friend and fight beside him in the Trojan War.

Eurytion, Eribotes, and Oileus

Eurytion, Eribotes, and Oileus all joined the quest. Oileus was a brave man who was skilled at chasing down and killing the enemy when they were retreating. Oileus was the father of a hero of the Trojan War: Little Ajax, who was also skilled at chasing down and killing the enemy when they were retreating.

Canthus

Canthus' father sent him to become one of the Argonauts, and Canthus was eager to join the quest. But Canthus would not return from the quest — he would not see his day of homecoming. Both he and the seer Mopsus were fated to die in Libya. Men may travel far, but Death is always able to find them. Death found Canthus and Mopsus in Libya, and they are buried there.

Clytius and Iphitus

Clytius and Iphitus joined the quest. Their father was a cruel man: Eurytus. Apollo, the god of archery, gave Eurytus a bow, but Eurytus became proud and challenged Apollo to an archery contest. Such challenges from mortals insult the gods, and Apollo killed Eurytus. Iphitus acquired the bow, and later he gave it as a guest-gift to Odysseus, who used the bow to kill the suitors in his palace after he returned from the Trojan War.

Telamon and Peleus

Telamon and Peleus were brothers; their father was Aeacus, King of Aegina, an island. However, they came to the city of Iolcus in Thessaly from separate places. They had killed their half-brother Phocus, and they had fled from Aegina to escape punishment. Telamon went to Salamis, an island, and lived there. Two of his sons — by different mothers — became important heroes of the Trojan War. Great Ajax was the most powerful Greek warrior with the exception of Achilles. Peleus went to Phthia. He married the immortal sea-nymph Thetis, of whom a prophecy had stated that she would give birth to a son who would be greater than his father. That son — the son of Peleus and Thetis — was the Greek Achilles, the greatest warrior of the Trojan War.

Butes and Phalerus

Butes, who loved battle, and Phalerus joined the quest. Phalerus' father, Alcon, had allowed him to join the quest, although his father had no other son who could look after him in his old age. Alcon wanted Phalerus to win glory. Both heroes were from Athens in Attica.

Theseus and Pirithous were Not Argonauts

Two important heroes did not join the quest. Both Theseus, King of Athens, and Pirithous, King of the Lapiths, were alive but held prisoner in the Land of the Dead. Pirithous was wedding Hippodamia when the Centaurs got drunk and tried to kidnap the human women. Pirithous, the other Lapiths, and his friend Theseus defeated the Centaurs. Pirithous married Hippodamia, who died shortly after giving birth to Polypoetes, who fought for the Greeks in the Trojan War. After the death of Hippodamia, Pirithous decided to seize Persephone and make her his bride, but Persephone was a goddess and she was married to Hades, King of the Land of the Dead. Pirithous and Theseus went to Tainaron, where was an entrance to the Underworld, and they journeyed down to the Land of the Dead, but when they sat down on a rock to rest, they discovered that they were trapped — they were unable to rise from the rock. Later, Heracles would rescue Theseus from the Land of the Dead, but the sin of Pirithous, who wanted to kidnap and marry a goddess who was already married to a god, was too great and Heracles was forced to leave him in the Land of the Dead.

Tiphys

Tiphys was the son of a sailor, and he had special skills. He knew when storms were coming, and he knew when it was safe to sail. He knew how to sail by the Sun, and he knew how to sail by the stars. Athena, goddess of wisdom, knew that his special skills would be necessary for the Argonauts, and she herself urged him to join the quest. Athena had given Argus the knowledge needed to build the *Argo*, and now she sent Jason a sailor with the knowledge needed to keep the ship safe. With such divine help, no one should wonder that the *Argo* became the best of all ships outfitted with oars.

Phlias

Phlias, a wealthy man, joined the quest.

Talaus, Areius, and Leodocus

Pero, the daughter of Neleus, gave birth to Talaus, Areius, and Leodocus, all of whom joined the quest. The seer Melampus helped his brother, Bias, to marry Pero. Neleus had demanded the cattle of a man named Iphiclus as the bride-price for Pero, and Melampus agreed to get the cattle for Neleus, although Melampus knew in advance that he would have to spend one year imprisoned in Iphiclus' cattle-stalls to get them. Melampus had acquired the ability to understand the speech of animals after two snakes he had saved from being killed licked his ears, and he heard two termites saying that the wood of the cattle-stall that Melampus was in was rotten and the cattle-stall would soon collapse. Melampus demanded to be moved, and shortly after he was moved, the cattle-stall collapsed, and his captors knew that he had special powers. He then cured Iphiclus of his childlessness, and brought the cattle of Iphiclus to Neleus.

Heracles

Heracles was not one to miss an adventure. He heard news of the gathering of heroes and immediately set out to join the quest, although he had finished only some of his famous Twelve Labors. Eurystheus, King of Mycenae, gave these labors to Heracles. Only by accomplishing these labors would Heracles be cleansed of a great sin he had committed: the murder of his children during an episode of madness that Hera had sent to him. Heracles' first labor was killing the Nemean lion. After he had been given this labor to accomplish, Heracles set out for Nemea and the lion. In Nemea, he met a shepherd named Molorchos whose son the lion had killed, and Heracles told him to wait thirty days. If Heracles returned with the carcass of the lion, then Molorchos would make a sacrifice to Zeus, but if Heracles had not returned with the lion's carcass in thirty days, that meant that Heracles was dead and Molorchos should make a sacrifice to Heracles — the Greeks and other ancient peoples sometimes made sacrifices to heroes as well as to gods. Heracles found the lion and tried to kill it by shooting arrows at it, but he discovered that weapons could not penetrate the lion's fur. Heracles forced the lion into its cave, which had two entrances. Heracles trapped the lion by blocking one entrance and then going into the cave through the other entrance. Because ordinary weapons could not penetrate the lion's skin, Heracles killed the lion by strangling it. To skin the lion, Heracles used one of the lion's claws. For the rest of his life, Heracles wore the skin of the lion. On the thirtieth day, he found Molorchos ready to make a sacrifice to Heracles, whom he thought had died, but Molorchos happily made the sacrifice to Zeus instead.

Another of Heracles' labors was capturing the Erymanthian boar. Boars are dangerous, and this especially dangerous boar lived on Mount Erymanthus. Heracles consulted the wise Centaur Chiron, seeking advice about how to capture the Erymanthian boar. Chiron advised Heracles to drive the Erymanthian boar into deep snow and then capture it. After following Chiron's advice, Heracles took the Erymanthian boar to Mycenae. Heracles heard of the upcoming voyage of the *Argo*, and he was in such a hurry to join the quest that he left the Erymanthian boar in the marketplace of Mycenae, instead of taking it to the palace of Eurystheus. Heracles did not ask permission from Eurystheus to join the quest.

Hylas

Hylas accompanied Heracles when he joined the quest. Hylas took care of Heracles' bow, and often he carried Heracles' arrows.

Nauplius

Nauplius joined the quest. He was descended from King Danaus, who was suspicious of Aegyptus and his fifty sons, who wanted to marry Danaus' fifty daughters, so he fled with his daughters, but Aegyptus and his fifty sons pursued them. To avoid a battle, Danaus told his fifty daughters to marry the fifty sons of Aegyptus, but although he allowed the marriages, he also ordered his fifty daughters to kill the fifty sons of Aegyptus. All of his daughters except Hypermnestra, who had married Lynceus, obeyed. Hypermnestra spared Lynceus because he treated her with respect and did not force her to have sex with him their first night together. The gods did not like what the forty-nine women who had killed their husbands had done, and so those forty-nine daughters are punished in Hades with meaningless work. They are condemned to spend all their time trying to fill up with water a container that has a big leak and so can never be filled. Only one daughter —Hypermnestra — avoided this eternal punishment.

Idmon

Idmon came from Argos to join the quest. He was the last of those from Argos to join the quest because he studied burnt offerings and the flight of birds, and his prophetic art had revealed to him that he would die during the quest. And yet he came and joined the quest so that he would win glory and fame.

Polydeuces and Castor

From Sparta came the twins Polydeuces and Castor. They were the brothers of Helen, the wife of King Menelaus of Sparta. Prince Paris from Troy would visit Menelaus and run away with Helen, who won fame as Helen of Troy. The Trojan War would be fought over Helen, who would look for her brothers from the high walls of Troy, but would not see them because by then they were dead and buried under the life-giving earth. Their mother, Leda, loved Polydeuces and Castor, and she sent them to join the quest to win glory and fame.

Lynceus and Idas

Lynceus and Idas, the sons of Aphareus, joined the quest. Idas lacked tact; he was outspoken and did not care when he insulted other people. Lynceus was reputed to have the finest eyesight of anyone in the entire world — he was reputed to be able to see things that were under the ground. Both Lynceus and Idas had great strength and great courage.

Periclymenus

Periclymenus joined the quest. His father was Poseidon, who gave him the ability to shapeshift and take the form of various animals such as an eagle. Poseidon also gave him great strength.

Amphidamas, Cepheus, and Ancaeus

Amphidamas, Cepheus, and Ancaeus joined the quest. Amphidamas and Cepheus were sons of Aleus, and Ancaeus was their nephew. Ancaeus' father, Lycurgus, was an older brother of Amphidamas and Cepheus. Lycurgus did not join the quest because he was growing old and he wanted to take care of Aleus, his father, a very old man. Ancaeus wore a bearskin, and his weapon was a two-edged axe. He had armor and other weapons, but his grandfather, Aleus, did not want him to join the quest and in an attempt to stop him had hidden the armor and weapons in a corner of a barn. These heroes came from Arcadia. Two Argonauts were named Ancaeus, and this Ancaeus was known as the Arcadian Ancaeus.

Augeias

Augeias, a wealthy man who was thought to be the offspring of Helios, god of the Sun, joined the quest. He wanted to see the land of Colchis and King Aeetes.

Asterius and Amphion

Asterius and Amphion, the sons of Hyperasius, joined the quest.

Euphemus

Euphemus' father was Poseidon, god of the sea, who granted him the ability to run on water. Euphemus was the fastest man in the world, and when he ran on water only his toes got wet. His mother was Europa.

Erginus and Ancaeus

Erginus and Ancaeus were also sons of Poseidon, and they also joined the quest. They lived in separate cities, but both were skilled at sailing ships and at fighting in battles. Two Argonauts were named Ancaeus, and this Ancaeus was known as Ancaeus, son of Poseidon.

Meleager, Laocoon, and Iphiclus

Meleager joined the quest, accompanied by his uncles Laocoon and Iphiclus. Laocoon was now an older man, and he served as Meleager's guardian. Iphiclus was younger, and he fought well hand to hand and was skilled at throwing the javelin. Meleager was scarcely out of boyhood. If he had been a year older so that he would have had more training, he likely would have been the most skilled and valuable Argonaut with the exception of Heracles.

Palaemonius

The real father of Palaemonius was the lame blacksmith god Hephaestus. Because of this, Palaemonius was also lame. But he had strong arms and shoulders and a broad chest, and he was tall and he had courage. No one criticized him.

Iphitus

Iphitus of Phocis had been Jason's host when Jason consulted the Delphic Oracle about the quest. Apollo, the god of prophecy, spoke through his priestess — known as the Pythia — at Delphi on the southwestern spur of Mount Parnassus in the valley of Phocis. Jason had gone to the Delphic Oracle to receive advice and information about the quest to acquire the Golden Fleece. In the Trojan War, two sons of Iphitus — Schedius and Epistrophus — led the warriors from their region. Two Argonauts had the name Iphitus; the other Iphitus used a bow that had come from Apollo.

Zetes and Calaïs

Zetes and Calaïs are known as the Boreads because their father was Boreas: the North Wind. Boreas had seen Oreithyia dancing on the banks of a river, and he had taken her away and slept with her. Her sons, Zetes and Calaïs, had feathered black wings with golden scales on their ankles, and they could fly. As they flew in the air, their black locks of hair streamed in the air.

Acastus

Acastus, the son of King Pelias himself, sought glory and fame, and he joined the quest.

Argus

Having built the *Argo*, Argus intended to sail on it and win glory and fame.

Jason and the Argonauts

These, then, were the men who sailed with Jason on the *Argo* in the quest to acquire the Golden Fleece. Many people called the Argonauts the Minyans because so many of them were descended from the daughters of Minyas, who had founded the city of Orchomenus in Boeotia. Jason himself was descended from Minyas' daughter Clymene, who was his maternal grandmother.

The *Argo* had been built and outfitted for the journey. The crew now stood around the ship, and many townspeople also stood there.

One townsman said what many people were thinking, "Zeus, what is King Pelias intending to do by sending Jason and the Argonauts to acquire the Golden Fleece? Is he intending for them to be exiled? This is a magnificent crew. If King Aeetes will not give them the Golden Fleece, Jason and the Argonauts can take it by force the first day they arrive at King Aeetes' palace. Still, Jason and the Argonauts must first get to King Aeetes' palace on the eastern shore of the Black Sea, and that journey will be difficult and dangerous."

The women lifted their hands into the air and prayed for a safe return of the Argonauts. Crying, one woman prayed, "Alcimede is now feeling sorrow at the end of her life because Jason, her son, is going on such a dangerous journey. And Jason's father, Aeson, also feels enormous grief. It would have been better for him if he had died and were now in his grave, unable to feel the grief that comes from knowing that his son will be in so much danger during the quest. If only Phrixus had perished with Helle in the Hellespont! If only the ram with the Golden Fleece had drowned there also! Then Jason's parents would not have to feel such overwhelming grief. Instead, Phrixus and the flying, talking ram with the Golden Fleece survived."

Many people were in the home of Jason's parents. Jason's mother, Alcimede, clung to his neck as she mourned. The female servants also mourned. Jason's father, now a very old man, groaned as he lay in bed.

Jason comforted his parents with soothing words, and he ordered the servants to pick up his weapons and other possessions to take them to the *Argo*.

Jason's mother continued to cling to him and mourn. She was like a young girl whose mother had died. She clings to her old nurse — her only friend — for comfort from the insults and meanness of her stepmother. For a long time, she cries so hard that she is unable to speak.

After Jason's mother had cried hard for a long time as she held him in her arms, she said, "I wish that I had died when King Pelias proclaimed that you would go forth to seek the Golden Fleece. If I had died, you would have buried me. That is the last kindness that you would have done for me. All other kindnesses you have already shown me — me who gave birth to you and who prevented you from being killed. But now I — who once was highly respected by women — shall live in a home without my only son. Artemis, the goddess of childbirth, did not allow me to have other sons. The ram with the Golden

Fleece saved the life of Phrixus, but now the ram brings great grief to me. I shall spend my time mourning you."

Alcimede wept, and her female servants wept with her.

Jason said, "Mother, please don't cry. Your tears will only make my quest more difficult. None of us knows what the gods have planned for us, and you must be courageous. We have much to be happy about. Athena has helped us to build the *Argo*, and the information that we have heard from the oracle of Apollo has all been good. Look also at the men who have assembled to come with me on my quest — these men are heroes. So do not cry; do not be an evil omen. I need to leave now."

Jason, looking like the god Apollo leaving his shrine at Delos, the island sacred to him, left the house and walked to the *Argo*. The townspeople came to watch him leave, and Iphias, the very old priestess of Artemis, protector of the city, kissed his right hand. She would have liked to speak to him, but he was in a hurry and quickly walked on. So often, the young leave behind the old.

Jason walked to the beach, where the Argonauts were waiting for him. King Pelias had not wanted Argus, the builder of the *Argo*, and Acastus, King Pelias' own son, to join the quest, but they defied his orders and came from the city to join Jason and the other Argonauts. Argus wore the hide of a black bull, and Acastus wore a double cloak that his sister had given to him.

All sat down on the ground, and Jason said to them, "The *Argo* is ready for the quest. All we need to set sail is a favorable wind. We will sail together to Colchis; we hope to be able to return home. But we have still one thing that needs to be done. We will work together, but we need to choose a leader. We ought not to show partiality to any one person, but instead choose the man who will be the best leader. The success of the quest will rest on the leader. We will meet strange men, and the leader will decide whether they are friendly or hostile."

Heracles sat in the middle of the Argonauts, and the young men looked at him and called on him to lead them. But Heracles said, "Do not ask me to be the leader. I will not accept the leadership. The only person who should be the leader is the man who brought all of us here. That man is Jason."

The men were impressed by Heracles' words, and they elected Jason leader.

Jason said to the men, "Let us do all that needs to be done. Let there be no further delay. We need to sacrifice to Apollo — he is the god who blesses

departures. I have already asked some servants to bring us cattle to sacrifice —
they are on the way. But now let us drag the *Argo* from off the shore to the
sea. Let us load the *Argo* and cast lots to determine who will sit where on the
rowing benches. And let us build an altar to Apollo on the beach; Apollo has
sent oracles that have promised to me that he will be our guide and help us if
we sacrifice to him."

Jason led by example and turned toward the work that needed to be done.
The other Argonauts quickly joined him. They examined the *Argo* and
strengthened it where needed. The sea would give the ship a pounding, and
they wanted it to be seaworthy.

Next the Argonauts dug a channel from the ship to the sea and placed
rollers in the bottom of the channel. They would push the ship on rollers until
it reached the sea. The Argonauts stood on both sides of the *Argo*. Tiphys, the
son of a sailor, gave the order to push and the Argonauts pushed the *Argo* to
the sea. Because of the friction of the *Argo*'s hull against the rollers, smoke rose
into the air. The *Argo* reached the sea, and the Argonauts stopped its forward
progress on holding on to ropes attached to the ship.

That accomplished, the Argonauts put the oars on the ship. They also put
the mast and sail on the ship, and they loaded the ship with provisions and
supplies.

Lots determined which men would sit on each bench; however, the middle
bench was the bench of honor and the Argonauts gave Heracles and the
Arcadian Ancaeus these seats of honor. Heracles wore his lionskin on the
bench, and the Arcadian Ancaeus wore his bearskin on the bench. No lots
were used to determine who would sit on the middle bench. In addition, the
Argonauts chose the experienced sailor Tiphys to serve as helmsman. He would
be the sailor at the helm who steered the ship.

They then built an altar on the shore in order to sacrifice to Apollo as god
of the shore and god of embarkations. Jason had earlier ordered his herdsmen
to bring two oxen to be sacrificed. His herdsmen now arrived, driving the oxen
in front of them. Some younger Argonauts drove the animals beside the altar,
and other Argonauts brought grains of barley and water.

Some of the Argonauts who would not kill the oxen threw grains of barley
on the oxen's heads; other Argonauts poured water on the oxen's heads. This
symbolized that they were also participating in the sacrifice although they were

not doing the killing. As the grains of barley fell and water poured on their heads, the oxen nodded, consenting to the sacrifice. All must consent to the sacrifice: Jason and the Argonauts, the god Apollo, and the two oxen.

Jason prayed to Apollo, "Hear me, Apollo. I consulted your oracle, and you promised to be my guide in this quest. Because of you, I am here now. I ask you to allow the *Argo* to reach Colchis and to return to Iolcus safely. I ask you to allow the Argonauts to reach Colchis and to return to Iolcus safely. When we return to Greece, we will again sacrifice to you — one bull for each Argonaut who safely returns to Greece. Accept this sacrifice from us to you — give us safe passage on this, the first voyage of the *Argo*. Give us good fortune, and give us good weather and a favorable wind."

Jason sprinkled some grains of barley. Heracles and the Arcadian Ancaeus had the honor of killing the oxen. Heracles used his club to hit one ox in the forehead. It collapsed. The Arcadian Ancaeus used his axe to cut through the neck sinews of the other ox. It fell. Other Argonauts cut the animals' throats. They skinned the oxen, and then they cut them up to be roasted. For Apollo, they cut out parts of the thighs, wrapped them in fat, and burnt them. Jason poured out wine that was unmixed with water as an offering to the god.

The prophet Idmon watched the sacrifice closely. The fires were burning well, and the dark smoke was rising as it should rise — Apollo had accepted the sacrifice.

Idmon then told the Argonauts some of what Apollo was planning: "The young men will return safely to Greece with the Golden Fleece, although we will have to face many challenges during our quest. I, however, will not return. I am fated to die and not return to Greece. Somewhere in Asia, my body will remain. For a long time, because of evil omens, I have known this. But I choose to go on this quest because I know that being an Argonaut will bring me fame and glory. People in my country and elsewhere will remember my name after I die."

The young Argonauts were happy at the good news of their safe return, but they grieved at the fate of Idmon.

They feasted at the sacrifice until shadows began to appear as the Sun sank to the horizon. The Argonauts rested on the shore, with lots of food and wine beside them, and they began to tell each other stories.

Jason, however, sat quietly, thinking of the hardships that they were sure to face on their quest. In doing so, he looked troubled.

Idas, who was outspoken and lacked tact, noticed Jason's troubled face and criticized him: "Jason, why do you look so troubled? Are you worried? Are you afraid? Are you a coward? Listen to me. I have a spear that I value highly — more highly than I value Zeus, king of gods and men. I swear that my spear and I will make this quest successful — even if a god should oppose us. I am your ally — your valuable ally."

Idas then drank deeply of wine that was unmixed with water — almost all Greeks mix their wine with water. The strong wine wet his lips and beard.

The other Argonauts cried out against Idas' blasphemy — the prophet Idmon most of all.

Idmon said to Idas, "Your words are foolish and reckless. You must have drunk too much strong wine. You have good qualities, but you are wrong when you insult the gods. If you are trying to encourage Jason, you are doing it in the wrong way. Avoid blasphemy! Remember the Aloadae — Otus and Ephialtes, two sons of Aloeus. They did not respect the gods. They wanted to pile mountains on top of mountains so that they could attack the gods and win goddesses to be wives for them. Otus wanted to marry the virgin goddess Artemis, and Ephialtes wanted to marry Hera, the wife of Zeus. Like you, Otus and Ephialtes were daring, but their quest ended in failure and death — Apollo killed them with his arrows."

Idas laughed at Idmon and said, "Be a prophet, and tell me how my life will end. Will my life be ended by a god, as were the lives of Otus and Ephialtes? Be sure that you truly forecast my end, or else plan how you will escape from me when I come after you should your prophecy be false."

Idas was angry, and his words were intended to infuriate Idmon. The quarrel would have escalated to physical acts of violence, but the Argonauts — Jason in the lead — intervened and stopped the quarrel.

Orpheus also intervened. He began to play the lyre and to sing. He sang of the beginning of the universe. In the beginning, all was chaos, and earth and sky and sea were mixed together, not separate. He sang about the strife that ended with the separation of earth and sky and sea. He sang about how the stars, the Moon, and the Sun received their appointed places in the heavens. He sang about the origin of mountains. He sang about the creation of streams and water-nymphs. He sang about the creation of four-legged animals. He sang about the earliest rulers on Mount Olympus — Ophion and Eurynome, the daughter of Ocean — and of how they were overthrown and Cronus supplanted Ophion and Rhea supplanted Eurynome. He sang of how Ophion and Eurynome fell into the Ocean waters, and he sang of how Cronus and Rhea ruled the giant Titans — who were themselves gods. He sang of the children of Zeus, the future king of gods and men, and of how Zeus lived in a cave in Mount Dicte on the island of Crete. Soon, Zeus would supplant his father, Cronus, but he did not yet possess the thunderbolts that the one-eyed Cyclopes would make for him. These formidable weapons would greatly increase Zeus' power.

Orpheus stopped singing, but mesmerized by his song, the Argonauts stayed silent with their heads still bent forward in a listening position. Soon, the Argonauts roused themselves and performed an act of piety to Zeus — they poured wine over the burning tongues of the sacrificed oxen. Then Jason and the Argonauts slept.

Tiphys awoke at dawn, and he quickly woke the others to prepare the oars for rowing. All were ready to set sail, and even the harbor and the *Argo* itself made sounds fitting for sea voyages. The *Argo*, given voice because of its beam that came from a tree that had grown in Dodona, where a shrine was dedicated to Zeus, shouted. The goddess Athena herself had put that beam in the ship.

The Argonauts sat on the benches that had been assigned to them. Their weapons were near each Argonaut. Heracles and the Arcadian Ancaeus sat on the middle bench, and the *Argo* sank a little deeper in the water because of Heracles' huge size. They untied the ropes used to moor the *Argo*, and some of the Argonauts poured wine into the sea as they prayed to the gods for a safe voyage.

Jason wept after he had looked at his homeland. He then looked at the sea, and Orpheus played the lyre as the other Argonauts rowed to open water. They rowed in time to the music of Orpheus, just as young men step in time to the music as they dance at a festival of Apollo at Delphi or at one of the other sites sacred to the god. The ends of the oars entered the water and created foam, and the metal armor of the Argonauts caught the rays of the Sun and glittered. The ship moved quickly, and a long wake formed behind it.

The embarkation of the *Argo* was a notable event, and the gods looked down at the *Argo* from their position on Mount Olympus. The nymphs of Mount Pelion admired the ship that Athena had helped build, and they admired the Argonauts and their rowing. The Centaur Chiron witnessed the setting off of the *Argo*. He waded into the sea and waved his hand at the Argonauts and wished them a safe journey and a happy homecoming. Chiron's wife also came. She lifted Achilles, the young boy whom Chiron was educating, high so that his father, Peleus, could see him.

Tiphys steered the *Argo* out of the harbor and into open water. Then the Argonauts raised the mast and the sail. A favorable wind filled the sail, and rowing was no longer necessary. The Argonauts relaxed as Orpheus entertained them with song. He sang about Artemis, who is the protector of ships and who sometimes roamed the lands that they were now passing. Fish heard the music and swam close by in the *Argo*'s wake. The fish were like sheep that follow a shepherd who plays a pipe as he leads them home at the end of a day in a pasture. The wind kept the *Argo* moving in the water.

Jason and the Argonauts sailed until they reached the coastline of Magnesia and the tomb of Dolops, a Thessalian hero who was a son of the god Hermes. The wind became unfavorable, and so Jason and the Argonauts beached the ship as darkness fell. In the darkness, they sacrificed sheep to honor the hero Dolops. They rested on the beach for two days, and then they set sail again.

As long as the wind was favorable, they sailed, both during the day and at night. They sailed past Mount Athos, and they continued to sail. But once they reached the island of Lemnos, the wind stopped.

The previous year, women had committed a great evil on Lemnos. The women had killed all the men. The married men had ignored their wives, instead choosing to sleep with women from Thrace whom they had seized in raids. The women of Lemnos had not given Aphrodite, the goddess of sexual passion, the honor she deserved, and so Aphrodite had punished the women in this way. The women of Lemnos had killed not only their husbands and the Thracian women they slept with, but they also killed every male inhabitant of Lemnos — the women were now afraid that they would be punished for their murders.

The only woman of Lemnos to allow a male to live was Hypsipyle, who would not kill her aged father, Thoas, the King of Lemnos. Instead, she put him in a chest and released it to drift over the sea. Hypsipyle hoped that someone would find the floating chest and save the life of her father. That is exactly what happened. Fishermen found the chest and released the king on the island then known as Oenoe. Thoas slept with the nymph named Oenoe, and they had a son whom they named Sicinus. Soon the island was given their son's name.

The women of Lemnos had taken over the work that the men had done. The women discovered that taking care of cattle, wearing armor, and plowing the fields was easier than doing the work that the women had done: weaving — work of which Athena is the patron goddess. However, the women of Lemnos were afraid that the Thracians would raid their island, and they watched the sea for signs of invading Thracian ships.

When the women of Lemnos saw the *Argo*, they thought that the Thracians were beginning an invasion, so they armed themselves and ran to the shore from the city. Hypsipyle dressed herself in her father's armor and went to join them on the shore. The women were silent and afraid.

Jason and the Argonauts landed on the shore, and they sent the diplomatic Aethalides, a herald, to talk to the women. Aethalides' father was Hermes, and Aethalides carried Hermes' scepter. Hermes had also given him an infallible memory. Even after Aethalides died, he kept his memory, unlike most of the heroes in the Land of the Dead. In addition, Aethalides was given the gift of residing alternately in the Land of the Dead and the Land of the Living after his death. Aethalides spoke to Hypsipyle, and diplomat that he was, he received her permission for the Argonauts to stay on the beach of Lemnos that night. But in the morning, an unfavorable breeze blew, and the Argonauts did not set sail.

Hypsipyle called an assembly of the women of Lemnos to decide what to do about the Argonauts. She stood before them and said, "Friends, I recommend that we give to the Argonauts gifts: food and wine and whatever else they need. If we treat them with generosity, they will not be our enemies. If we give them what they need, they can stay by their ship and will not need to enter our city. If they become close to us, they may find out that we have killed all the males of Lemnos. If they learn that, the news of our crime will spread elsewhere, and we will be punished for what we have done. That is what I recommend, but I want to hear what you think. That is why I have called this assembly."

Hypsipyle sat on her father's throne, and her aged nurse, Polyxo, stood up — something that was hard for her to do. Her feet hurt, and she leaned on a staff, but she was determined to speak. Behind the aged white-haired nurse sat four young women, still virgins. Polyxo went to the center of the women and raised her head with difficulty. She said, "Hypsipyle is correct. We ought to help the Argonauts. It is better to make friends than enemies. But we need to think about the future. The Thracians are a danger to us. Either they or other enemies could appear suddenly, just as the *Argo* appeared suddenly. But even if we are not attacked, we have other troubles to think about. We all will get older. Aged women such as myself will die off despite the care you give us. What will happen to you young women when you get old if you have no children to take care of you? Who will do the plowing? Who will do the reaping? Death has not yet arrived for me, but I expect to die sometime in the coming year. I will die before you young women become old. You young women need to think about the future. Men have arrived here on the *Argo*. The men can be your salvation. Are you willing to let these men have your homes, your herding animals, and your city? If the men chose to live here, they can give you children."

The women of Lemnos liked Polyxo's plan to have the men come into their city and into their homes. Hypsipyle stood up and said to the women, "Then it is agreed to follow the advice of Polyxo. I will send a messenger to the ship to invite the Argonauts into the city."

Hypsipyle said to Iphinoe, her herald, "Go to the *Argo* and talk to the captain. Tell him to come to my palace to hear good news. And let his men know that they can land safely and come into the city without fear. They will be our friends."

Iphinoe went to the *Argo* and told Jason and the Argonauts, "Hypsipyle, the daughter of Thoas, requests that the captain of the *Argo* come to her to hear good news. You Argonauts may land safely — immediately, if you wish — and come into the city as our friends."

The Argonauts were in favor of Iphinoe's words. They assumed that King Thoas must have died and that his daughter, Hypsipyle, must have taken over and was ruling as Queen of Lemnos. They wanted Jason to see Hypsipyle immediately. They would attend to the beaching of the *Argo* and then enter the city.

Jason dressed for the occasion. He wore a purple cloak that the goddess Athena herself had made. As Argus, Jason, and the Argonauts were building the *Argo* and Athena was decreeing the measurements of the ship, she took time off to give Jason this cloak of double width. It was red in the center and purple at the edges and brighter than the Sun at dawn. On the ends of the cloak were embroidered works of realistic art.

On the cloak were depicted the Cyclopes making a thunderbolt for Zeus. The thunderbolt was nearly completed, but it still lacked one ray that the Cyclopes were pounding with iron hammers on an anvil.

On the cloak were depicted two sons of Antiope — Amphion and Zethus, the builders of the walls of the city of Thebes. The cloak showed the two men building the walls of Thebes with boulders. With great difficulty, Zethus lifted a boulder as big as a mountain peak, but Amphion played a lyre that the god Hermes had given him and as he played it a boulder twice as big as the boulder that Zethus carried followed him.

On the cloak were depicted longhaired Aphrodite and the shield of Ares, the god of war, with whom she was having an affair. The left side of her tunic had slipped down, revealing her breast. Aphrodite's image was mirrored in the shiny metal of Ares' shield.

On the cloak was depicted a raiding party. Taphian raiders fought the sons of Electryon. The Taphians had wanted a share of Electryon's kingdom, but Electryon refused their request, and the Taphians became raiders and stole his cattle. Electryon's sons resisted them, but the pasture became bloody, and the Taphians defeated the greatly outnumbered sons of Electryon.

On the cloak was depicted the chariot race in which Pelops won the right to marry Hippodamia. (This Hippodamia is different from the Hippodamia who married Pirithous, King of the Lapiths.) Her father, Oenomaus, had heard a prophecy that his son-in-law would kill him. He decreed that each of Hippodamia's suitors would have to compete against him in a chariot race. If the suitor won, he would marry Hippodamia. If the suitor lost, Oenomaus would kill him. Oenomaus had killed thirteen suitors before Pelops competed in the chariot race, but Pelops switched the sturdy linchpins attaching the wheels to Oenomaus' chariots with linchpins that would break. During the race, in which Pelops took the lead, the linchpins broke just as Oenomaus was about to spear Pelops in the back. Oenomaus fell from the chariot and was dragged to his death, and then Pelops was able to marry Hippodamia.

The cloak also depicted a very young Apollo defending his mother, Leto, as the giant Tityos attempted to carry her away. Apollo shot arrows at Tityos and killed him. For his arrogance at attempting to kidnap and rape the goddess Leto, Tityos is punished in the Land of the Dead by two vultures that forever eat his liver. Tityos had two mothers. His first mother was Elara. His father, Zeus, slept with Elara and made her pregnant and then hid her deep underground so that his jealous wife, Hera, would not learn about his affair. Tityos, a giant, grew so large that he split Elara's womb. His second mother — Gaia, the Earth — carried him to term.

The cloak also depicted Phrixus and the ram with the Golden Fleece. The ram appeared to be speaking and Phrixus listening, and the figures were depicted so realistically that people looking at the figures would listen intently for a long time in an effort to hear the words of the ram.

This is the cloak that Jason wore — a gift from Athena. In his right hand was another gift — a light spear that the huntress Atalanta had given to him. She was a virgin who did not wish to marry, and she had asked Jason to allow her to become an Argonaut. He had declined her request because he feared the troubles that could result from a single young woman journeying on a ship filled with men.

Jason walked to the city. He looked like the bright evening star that brides-to-be look at from their chambers as they long for the grooms that their parents have promised — grooms who are still in a distant land.

As he entered the city, the women — who had been without men for so long — came out to look at him. Jason kept his eyes on the ground and walked directly to the palace of Hypsipyle. Maids opened the doors for him, and Iphinoe led him to Hypsipyle.

Hypsipyle, still a virgin, blushed. She spoke to Jason, and some of what she said about the lack of men in Lemnos was not true: "Welcome. You have come to a city without men. They have left Lemnos and are now plowing the fields of Thrace. Let me tell you true things. Let me tell you why the men left Lemnos. Under my father, the then-King Thoas, the men of Lemnos were accustomed to make raids on Thrace and bring back cattle and other booty and women to serve as slaves. But Aphrodite was displeased by the actions of the men, and she punished them by removing their sense of right and wrong. The men hated their lawfully wedded wives, and they forced their wives out of their homes. The men then slept with their Thracian slave-women. The women of Lemnos waited, hoping that the men would recover their sense of right and wrong. That did not happen. Instead, the evil increased. The men ignored their legitimate daughters. Instead, they raised a new generation of bastard children. Legitimate wives and their legitimate daughters wandered the streets without a home to go to. Fathers ignored their legitimate daughters and did not care when a cruel stepmother mistreated a daughter or even caused her death. Sons did not protect mothers. Brothers did not protect sisters. The men cared for no females except for their slave-women.

"Inspired by a god, we women of Lemnos took action. While the men were away on yet another raiding trip to Thrace, we shut the city-gates against them, and when they returned, we would not let them into the city. We wanted them to regain their sense of right and wrong — or move elsewhere. They asked for their sons, and we gave the men their sons. Now the men make their living in Thrace.

"You are welcome to live here. If you choose to live here, you can be King of Lemnos and carry my father's scepter. Lemnos is not a poor land. It has rich soil — soil that is richer than the soil of any of the islands in the Augean Sea. Go to your ship and tell your men that they are welcome to live here. Feel free to come into the city at any time."

Hypsipyle did not tell Jason what had really happened to the males of Lemnos.

Jason said, "Hypsipyle, thank you for your welcome and for your help. I will tell my men what you have told me. But be aware that we will not live here permanently. We have a dangerous quest to accomplish."

He gently touched her right hand and left. Again, young women who had not seen a man for a long time surrounded him as he walked through the streets of the city. The young women danced around him.

Jason told the Argonauts what Hypsipyle had told him. As he was talking, young women arrived with gifts for the Argonauts. They were eager to know the Argonauts, and the Argonauts went with them to their homes. Aphrodite, the goddess of sexual desire, filled the young women and the Argonauts with desire for each other. The island of Lemnos was dedicated to Hephaestus, and Aphrodite wanted to please Hephaestus by repopulating his island with children.

Jason went to the home of Hypsipyle, and the other Argonauts went to the homes of the other young women, but by choice Heracles and a few of his friends stayed by the *Argo*. The city was filled with dancing and feasts and sacrifices to Hephaestus and Aphrodite.

Jason and the Argonauts stayed on Lemnos for several days and may have never left except that Heracles became impatient to continue their quest. Heracles called a meeting of men only and said, "For what reason did we leave Iolcus? Were we exiled because we killed some men? Were we exiled because we killed relatives? Did we leave Iolcus and come to Lemnos so that we could find wives for ourselves? Did we come to Lemnos so that we could plow the fields and the women? We will win no glory if we choose to stay here. We will win glory only by getting the Golden Fleece, and no miracle will make the Golden Fleece come to Lemnos. If we want the Golden Fleece, we have to go and get it. Perhaps we should give up, leave Lemnos, and sail back to Iolcus. We can leave Jason here to sleep with Hypsipyle and win glory by repopulating Lemnos through his own efforts."

All were shamed by Heracles' criticisms. The meeting ended, and the men prepared to continue their quest. The women of Lemnos quickly learned of the men's plan to leave, and they came to the men. The women grieved, but they did not ask the men to stay. They were like bees coming out of their hive and going to the meadow to swarm around flowers. The women prayed that the men would have a safe journey. They touched the men lovingly and said kind words to them.

Crying, Hypsipyle held Jason's hands and said to him, "May the gods help you to obtain the Golden Fleece and take it to Iolcus. That is your quest. That is what you hope to accomplish. If you ever choose to return to Lemnos, my father's scepter will be waiting for you. You can bring with you people to populate this island. But I believe that you will never return to Lemnos — you have other things you wish to do. However, please remember me wherever you go. And tell me what I should do if the gods allow me to give birth to a boy of yours."

Jason replied, "Hypsipyle, thank you for your gracious prayers. I hope that the gods will answer them. Don't be angry at me if I choose to live in my own country — King Pelias permitting. I do hope that the gods will help me during this quest. But if I should not return from this quest, and if you bear me a boy, please send him when he is old enough to Iolcus to my parents. If they are still alive, my son can console them and take care of them in their old age."

Jason and the Argonauts boarded the *Argo*. They took their places at the oars, and they rowed out to sea.

That evening, Orpheus suggested that they land on the island of Samothrace, which is dedicated to Electra, the daughter of Atlas, the Titan who holds up the celestial sphere. Orpheus knew that on Samothrace the Argonauts could undergo a secret initiation and learn secret rites that would assist them in their quest. Such secret rites must not be described in writing.

They sailed again and eventually arrived at the beginning of the Hellespont, which would lead them to the Sea of Marmara. All night they sailed through the Hellespont, and by dawn they had sailed into the Sea of Marmara. They would sail this sea and then sail up the Bosphorus until they reached the Clashing Rocks. Once past the Clashing Rocks, they would be in the Black Sea.

They landed at the place where the Doliones lived under King Cyzicus. Near the Doliones lived a people who each had six arms. Two arms sprang from the Doliones' shoulders, and four more arms sprang from their sides. The Doliones were descended from Poseidon, and the god kept them safe from the six-armed people, who lived on the Mountain of the Bears.

At the advice of Tiphys, the Argonauts replaced their small anchor-stone with a much larger and more suitable one. They left the small anchor-stone at the spring of Artacie; later, at the command of Apollo, this small anchor-stone was taken to a temple of Athena and treated with respect because it was a relic of the voyage of the *Argo*.

King Cyzicus and the Doliones greeted Jason and the Argonauts and treated them as friends and gave them hospitality. They built an altar and sacrificed to Apollo, the god who protects those who disembark. King Cyzicus gave them wine and sheep — he obeyed an oracle that told him to treat these strangers as friends.

King Cyzicus, a young man, resembled Jason, and neither had children. King Cyzicus did have a wife, Cleite, but she had not yet given birth. In fact, they were newlyweds. He had paid a large dowry to her father, and then he had brought her to his country. King Cyzicus left his wife in their home, and he feasted with Jason and the Argonauts. King Cyzicus asked them about their quest, and they asked him about the lands and seas they must travel. He told them all he knew, but they still wished to know more than he could tell them.

In the morning, some of the older Argonauts climbed up Mount Dindymon to see what they could of the path the *Argo* must take. Heracles and the younger Argonauts stayed by the *Argo*.

The race of six-armed people now tried to trap the *Argo* in the harbor by throwing into the water boulders to stop the ship from leaving. Heracles, however, shot arrows at them and killed many of the six-armed people. The remaining six-armed people threw rocks at him. Hera seemed to want this to be yet another of Heracles' famous Labors. The Argonauts who were climbing Mount Dindymon saw what was happening and came down to assist Heracles and the younger Argonauts. In the battle, all of the six-armed people were killed.

Woodcutters sometimes cut wood for a ship's hull and let the boards lie on the beach in rows. The dead six-armed people looked like those boards. Some had only their heads and chests in the water; some had only their legs in the water. Either way, they were food for fish and birds — both at the same time. The Argonauts were now safe.

They set sail and made good time, but then the wind turned against them and drove them back to the land of King Cyzicus and the Doliones. They landed the *Argo* there that night, but because of darkness they did not realize whose land they were on. And because of darkness, King Cyzicus and the Doliones did not realize that friends had landed. They feared that enemies had come to make raids on their land. Therefore, King Cyzicus and the Doliones put on their armor and attacked. Both sides fought, not realizing that they were fighting friends. The battle was like a forest fire feeding on dry brushwood.

King Cyzicus was fated to die that night: No one can evade his or her fate. Mortals are like trapped birds. Jason fought him and speared him in the chest, shattering the breastbone. King Cyzicus sank to the ground and died. He had obeyed the oracle and treated the Argonauts as friends, but nevertheless Jason killed him and the Argonauts killed many of his people.

Heracles killed Telecles and Megabrontes.

Acastus, the son of King Pelias, killed Sphodris.

Peleus, the father of Achilles, killed Zelys and Gephyrus.

Telamon, the father of Great Ajax, killed Basileus.

Idas, who was outspoken and lacked tact, killed Promeus.

Clytius killed Hyacinthus.

The twins Castor and Polydeuces, the brothers of Helen, who would become Helen of Troy, killed Megalossaces and Phlogius.

Meleager killed Itymoneus and Artaces.

The Doliones still honor their fallen heroes.

The rest of the Doliones fled back to their city — they were like doves fleeing from a fierce hawk. Soon their city was filled with loud lamentations for the dead.

At dawn, more grief arrived: Both sides realized that they had been battling friends. Jason and the Argonauts mourned when they saw King Cyzicus, who had treated them so well, lying dead and bloody. The Argonauts and the Doliones mourned King Cyzicus for three days, and then they put him in a burial mound and held funeral games in his honor.

King Cyzicus' newlywed wife, Cleite, did not want to face life without him. She hanged herself with a rope. In addition to the Doliones, the woodland nymphs mourned her death, and they cried so many tears that the tears created a spring that is named after Cleite.

That day was the worst day for the Doliones: both men and women. No one could eat, and when they did begin to eat again, they lived on food that did not need to be cooked because no one wanted to make the effort to grind their grain at home. When the Doliones later remembered their dead at anniversaries, they did not grind their grain at home but instead ground it at a public mill.

For twelve days, the winds were unfavorable and Jason and the Argonauts could not depart. One night, Acastus and Mopsus stood guard over the Argonauts. Near dawn, a sea bird known as a halcyon flew to the *Argo* and hovered over the head of Jason and cried out. The cries of the halcyon imparted knowledge to Mopsus, who had prophetic powers.

Mopsus awoke Jason and told him, "I have heard a bird-sign, and I know what you need to do to stop these unfavorable winds. Climb to the top of the mountain here and sacrifice to Rhea, the mother of the gods. She has dominion over winds and sea, and Zeus respects her, as do the other gods. All gods defer to Rhea."

Mopsus' words made Jason happy. He quickly arose and woke the other Argonauts to give them the good news that Mopsus had told him. Some Argonauts stayed behind to guard the *Argo*, but the others climbed the mountain, bringing cattle with them for a sacrifice. From the top of the mountain, they could see a great distance. They found an old stump of a massive vine and cut it out. Argus carved it into an image of the goddess Rhea, and then they made an altar to Rhea. They prayed to her and Titias and Cyllenus, who sit beside her and who are known to be guiders of destiny. Titias and Cyllenus are of the race of the Dactyls, to whom the nymph Anchiale gave birth in a cave on Mount Dicte on the island of Crete.

Jason prayed to Rhea to send the unfavorable winds elsewhere, and he poured libations on the burning sacrifice. Orpheus commanded the young Argonauts to dance in full armor and to hit their swords against their shields so that the noise would drown out the lamentations of the Doliones as they grieved for their dead king — the lamentations were evil omens.

Rhea approved the sacrifice. The trees grew fruit, the grass grew at their feet, and wild beasts wagged their tails and came to the Argonauts. No water had been available on Mount Dindymon, but now a stream of water gushed at Rhea's command.

Jason and the Argonauts then held a feast to honor Rhea, and they sang in honor of her. The unfavorable wind died down, and they departed from the land of the Doliones. They competed as they rowed, seeing who would be the last to tire of the rowing. The wind had gone, and it was up to the Argonauts to propel the *Argo* forward. In their competition, they made the *Argo* go so fast that not even the horses of Poseidon could outrun it.

Eventually, the waters grew rougher and most of the Argonauts grew exhausted and Heracles did the majority of the rowing. The strokes of his oar made the *Argo* shiver. But Heracles rowed so hard that his oar broke in two, and he fell sideways. Half of his oar remained in his hand, and half of his oar floated away. Heracles was angry. He preferred to work when work needed to be done.

That evening, Jason and the Argonauts pulled up on shore. It was the time when a farmer goes home, dirty and exhausted from working in the fields, and looks at his calloused hands and curses the stomach that makes him work so hard to keep it filled.

Because Jason and the Argonauts had no hostile intentions, the inhabitants of the land received them with kindness and gave them sheep and wine. Some of the Argonauts busied themselves with collecting leaves for bedding and wood for fire. Some mixed the wine for the feast that would follow the sacrifice.

Heracles, however, went into the woods to find a pine tree from which to make himself an oar. He looked for and found a young pine tree of the right height and without too many branches. He put down his bow and arrows, and he used his club to hit the pine tree and loosen it. He then spread his legs wide apart, grasped the pine tree with his strong hands, and although it was deep rooted, he tore it by its roots from the ground. He was like a squall wind pulling away a mast from a ship. Heracles picked up the tree and his weapons, and he headed back to the Argonauts' camp.

Meanwhile, Heracles' young companion and armor keeper, Hylas, went to a spring to get water for the evening meal. Hylas served Heracles, and Heracles had taught him to be a good servant. Hylas' father was Theiodamas, King of the Dryopes, an unjust and evil people. Heracles wanted to punish the Dryopes, so when he found Theiodamas using two oxen to plow a field, he started a quarrel with Theiodamas over one of the oxen, saying that he was out of food and wanted to butcher the ox, and he killed Theiodamas. Since that time, Heracles had raised Hylas.

Hylas found a spring, reaching it at a time when nymphs — minor female nature deities — gathered together to dance in honor of Artemis. Most of the nymphs were a short distance away, but one naiad — the nymph of the spring — saw Hylas and fell in love with him. Hylas knelt to put his pitcher in the water. The naiad reached one hand up to draw Hylas' head down so she could kiss him, and with her other hand she drew Hylas into the spring.

Polyphemus had left the camp of the Argonauts to try to find Heracles. He heard the startled Hylas cry out. He ran to the spring as if he were a hungry wild animal running toward sheep so it can feast on them. But like a wild animal that is forced to stay hungry because the shepherds have penned up the sheep, Polyphemus was disappointed because he could not find Hylas. Polyphemus shouted, but Hylas did not answer.

Polyphemus drew his sword — he was afraid that evil men or wild animals had attacked and killed Hylas. Holding his sword, and shouting for Hylas, he met Heracles, who had heard him shouting.

Polyphemus said to Heracles, "I have terrible news! Hylas went out for water. I heard him cry out. Evil men or wild animals may have killed him."

Angry, Heracles threw the pine tree down and started running like a bull that the sting of a horsefly has maddened. The bull does care about the herdsmen; it cares only about its pain. It runs and runs, stopping only to bellow in its pain. Heracles ran a long time, and then he stopped to shout for Hylas.

The morning star rose, and so did the wind. It was good sailing weather, and Tiphys urged Jason and the Argonauts to board ship and continue the quest. In the darkness, no one realized that Hylas, Heracles, and Polyphemus were missing. They sailed away with their sail full of wind.

But when dawn arrived and banished the darkness, they realized that Hylas, Heracles, and Polyphemus were missing. Heracles, in particular, would be missed — he was the strongest and the bravest Argonaut. The Argonauts argued over whether they should or should not return and find the missing Argonauts. Jason sat quietly, mourning and not taking a side.

Enraged, Telamon said to Jason, "You are sitting quietly. You must be happy because Heracles is not here. You must have planned to leave Heracles behind so that his fame would not eclipse your own in this quest. But why should I talk to you? We need to return and get Heracles, no matter what you and any friends of yours think."

Telamon ran at the pilot of the *Argo*, Tiphys, and he would have taken over as pilot and set a course back to where they had left Heracles behind, although it meant fighting the wind, but Zetes and Calaïs, the sons of the North Wind, stopped Telamon. This action would later cost them their lives. Heracles, angry that he had been left behind, would kill Zetes and Calaïs at the funeral of King Pelias. Heracles would build for them a burial mound and set on top of it two pillars, one of which would amaze witnesses who saw it bend when the North Wind blew.

But now the sea-god Glaucus, a messenger of the sea-god Nereus, came out of the water and held on to the side of the *Argo*. He said, "Why do you want to bring Heracles on this quest? He has a different fate. He must perform his Twelve Labors for the cruel Eurystheus. Only a few remain to be done, and if he succeeds in performing them, he will become an immortal god.

"Polyphemus also has a fate different from going on this quest. He will found a famous city and die soon afterward.

"Hylas, whom Heracles and Polyphemus are seeking, is also well. A naiad has fallen in love with him and made him her husband."

Glaucus then plunged into the water and disappeared.

The Argonauts were happy to hear this news, and Telamon apologized to Jason. Telamon grabbed Jason's hand and kissed him and said, "Please do not be angry at me. My anger made me blind. I apologize for what I said. I hope that the wind will blow away my unwise words, and that you and I, who have been friends, will be friends again."

Jason was willing for Telamon and him to again be friends: "You did insult me by saying that I betrayed one of my friends, and that hurt, but I understand that you did that because of your concern for a man who is your friend. You were not quarreling with me about something unimportant, like a flock of sheep. I hope that if need be you will do for me what you did for Heracles."

The quarrel was over, and Telamon and Jason were friends again.

Zeus turned his attention to Polyphemus and to Heracles. Polyphemus would found a city in the land of Mysia, the land where Hylas married the naiad. Heracles would complete his Twelve Labors.

Heracles searched for Hylas, but he could not find him. He ordered the people of Mysia to find out what had happened to Hylas, threatening to make war against them if they failed. He wanted to know whether Hylas was alive or dead. The Mysians promised to search for Hylas and gave Heracles some of their young men as hostages. The Mysians swore never to give up the search for Hylas. Even now, they seek information about him. They also are on good terms with the people of the city of Trachis, which is where Heracles left his hostages.

The *Argo* sailed all night. In the morning, the wind died, but Jason and the Argonauts saw a wide beach, and they rowed to it and went ashore.

Chapter 2: The Argo Journeys to Colchis

Amycus, an arrogant man, ruled this land — the land of the Bebryces. Here he had farms and cattle. His father was Poseidon. Amycus challenged arrivals to his country to a boxing match. An excellent boxer, he had killed many men in his bouts.

Amycus and some armed Bebryces went to the *Argo*. They did not ask who Jason and the Argonauts were or where they were going. They did not give Jason and the Argonauts hospitality. Instead, Amycus said, "Sailors, know that anyone who lands here will not be allowed to continue their journey until one of them has boxed me. Pick your best boxer and let him and me fight here and now. If you do not do this willingly, we will force you to do it."

All of the Argonauts were infuriated by the words of Amycus, Polydeuces — the best of all boxers, with the exception of Heracles — most of all. Polydeuces stepped forward and said, "I don't know who you are, but I accept your challenge. Let's fight."

Amycus stared at him. Amycus was like a lion that a hunter has wounded. Many hunters are near the lion, but the lion stares only at the hunter who wounded him but failed to kill him.

Polydeuces took off his cloak, a gift from one of the women of Lemnos. Amycus also threw his cloak and his staff on the ground. They looked for a good spot to box, and they then told their friends to sit on the ground in different spots.

Amycus and Polydeuces were different physically. Amycus made people think he resembled the hideous offspring of hideous monsters. The goddess Gaia became angry at Zeus because he had imprisoned the Titans, to whom she had given birth. Therefore, Gaia gave birth to Typhoeus, the Father of All Monsters. Typhoeus married Echidna, the Mother of All Monsters. Typhoeus fought Zeus and lost.

Polydeuces, in contrast, resembled a brightly shining star of Heaven. He was the son of Zeus, and he was a young man with his first beard on his cheeks, although his body and fighting spirit were growing strong like those of a wild animal.

Polydeuces shadowboxed to make sure that his arms had not been adversely affected by all the rowing that he had done on the *Argo*. Amycus simply stood silently, watching Polydeuces and anticipating making him bleed.

Lycoreus, who served Amycus, placed two pairs of rawhide gauntlets before Polydeuces and Amycus, who said, "Take your pick of the pairs of gauntlets. We need not cast lots. I don't want you to think that you have been cheated. After we box, you can tell your friends how skilled I am at drawing blood."

Polydeuces simply smiled and did not reply. He picked up the pair of gauntlets nearest to him, and his twin brother Castor and his fellow Argonaut Talaus tied the gauntlets over his hands. At the same time, Amycus' warriors Aretus and Ornytus did the same thing for Amycus. Aretus and Ornytus did not know that this was the last time they would bind gauntlets on the hands of Amycus.

Gauntlets bound, the two men moved closer and started to fight. A big wave can threaten a ship, but a skilled pilot can evade the full force of the wave and save the ship. Amycus was like the big wave, ever threatening destruction to Polydeuces, who like the skilled pilot evaded the full force of his blows.

Polydeuces watched Amycus' moves, looking for both strengths and weaknesses. Having sized up his opponent, Polydeuces started fighting in full force instead of engaging in defensive maneuvers. The two men stood and hit each other, and the pounding of their blows and the grinding of their teeth were like the hammering of shipwrights as they build a boat.

When Polydeuces and Amycus were both exhausted, they backed away from each other and breathed deeply and wiped away their sweat. Then they fought again, just like two bulls fighting to see who would mate with a young heifer.

Amycus now attempted to land a killing blow on Polydeuces' head, but Polydeuces turned aside and the blow fell on his shoulder as he hit Amycus above the ear and crushed the bones. Amycus fell, the Argonauts shouted in triumph, and Amycus died.

Furious at the death of their king, the Bebryces picked up their weapons and charged at Polydeuces, eager to spear or club him to death. But the Argonauts drew their swords and stood in front of Polydeuces, eager to protect him.

Polydeuces' twin brother, Castor, made the first kill. As a warrior rushed at him, Castor swung his sword with such force that the warrior's head was cut into two halves that fell upon the warrior's shoulders.

Polydeuces also fought. He ran and jumped at Itymoneus and kicked him and knocked him to the ground. When Mimas attacked him, Polydeuces hit him above his left eyebrow and tore away the eyelid, leaving the eyeball uncovered.

The Bebryces wounded some of the Argonauts. Oreides wounded Talaus, cutting the skin of his side with a spear. Aretus clubbed Iphitus, son of the archer Eurytus, who was not yet fated to die.

Sword drawn, Clytius rescued Iphitus by cutting down his attacker.

The Arcadian Ancaeus wrapped a black bearskin around his arm to use as a shield, and raising his two-headed axe, he fiercely fought the enemy. Telamon and Peleus fought beside him, and Jason charged the Bebryces.

Grey wolves can sneak past shepherds and dogs and enter a pen filled with sheep. The wolves look at the frightened sheep and choose which to attack and carry away, and the sheep can do nothing but be afraid and huddle together. The Argonauts made the Bebryces feel the kind of fear that such sheep feel.

The Bebryces fled. Beekeepers or shepherds can smoke bees in their hive. At first, the bees are angry and buzz, but eventually they fly away from the smoke. The Bebryces were like those bees.

The Bebryces fled inland, and they told everyone that Amycus had died. Although they were not aware of it yet, they had more to suffer. The Bebryces' neighboring enemies — the Mariandyni — were attacking their villages and vineyards. For generations, the Bebryces and the Mariandyni had fought over this land, which was valuable because of its iron. At the same time, the Argonauts were raiding the Bebryces' sheep.

The Argonauts thought about the cowardice of the Bebryces and wondered what would have happened if Heracles had been present. A young Argonaut said, "If Heracles had been here, Amycus would not have challenged the best of the Argonauts to fight him. He would have looked at Heracles' club and decided to be friendly to us Argonauts. We made a mistake when we left Heracles behind. We should have gone back for him." But all that had happened had been what Zeus wanted to happen.

Jason and the Argonauts stayed there that night and took care of the wounded and sacrificed to the gods. All stayed awake to eat and drink. They celebrated the victory of Polydeuces' boxing match with song, and they made laurel wreaths for all to celebrate their victory over the Bebryces.

At dawn, they loaded the *Argo* with their spoils, and they set sail. A huge wave came toward them and seemed about to engulf and sink the ship, but the skill of their pilot, Tiphys, saved them. They kept sailing, and the following day, they landed on the coast of the land where Phineus lived.

Phineus was a prophet through the gift of Apollo, but he had misused his special insight. He knew the will of Zeus, and when he revealed the will of Zeus to Humankind, he held nothing back. Zeus permits prophets to reveal part of his will, but not all.

Because of Phineus' misuse of his special insight, Zeus punished him by making him blind in his long-lasting old age. Zeus even made sure that Phineus was not able to enjoy the delicacies that neighbors brought him when they wished him to use his prophetic ability. Every time that Phineus attempted to eat, bird-like Harpies swooped down from the sky and devoured much of the food and fouled all the rest. They snatched the food from his plate and his hands. Everything that the Harpies touched stank. Only a starving man could bear to come near the food the Harpies left behind. The Harpies left for Phineus only enough food to keep Phineus from starving to death; they wanted him to continue to live and to be tormented.

But Zeus had decided that Phineus' punishment would eventually come to an end. When Phineus heard the voices and footsteps of Jason and the Argonauts, he knew that these were the men who Zeus had told him would end his torment. Soon, he would be allowed to eat his fill of good food. Phineus rose from bed, grabbed his cane, and walked to Jason and the Argonauts, touching the walls of his home to guide himself.

Phineus was old and withered, and his limbs trembled, and his body was shriveled and dirty. He was so weak that he fainted in front of the Argonauts, who gathered around him.

Making a great effort, Phineus said, "You have travelled here on the *Argo* — this I know because of the prophetic ability that Apollo gifted to me. Miserable as I am, I still thank Apollo for his gift. I ask you in the name of Zeus, the name of Apollo, and the name of Hera — the goddess who sent you on your quest —

to help me. I ask you not to continue on your quest without first having helped me.

"I am blind, I am old, I am miserable, and I am cursed with Harpies who come from I don't know where — it is a place beyond mortal understanding — and swoop down on me and eat my food before I can taste it. I can do nothing to stop these Harpies. I cannot escape from them because they are so swift — I could sooner forget my hunger. Any food they leave for me stinks and no person less hungry than I could bear to even come near it, much less eat it. But I have no choice; I must eat it. That is the only food that the Harpies allow me to eat.

"But I know of an oracle that states that the two sons of the North Wind will free me from the Harpies. They are famous, and nobody unknown will be able to help me. This I know because I am Phineus, and I have prophetic power. I am the son of Agenor, and I married Cleopatra, whose father is Boreas, the North Wind. She is the sister of the two sons of the North Wind. She was my first wife. I used to rule Thrace, and I was wealthy."

The Argonauts, and especially the two sons of the North Wind, Zetes and Calaïs, pitied Phineus. Zetes and Calaïs went to Phineus. Zetes held the old man's hands and said to him, "I doubt that anyone on earth has to bear more hardship than you do. Why are you being persecuted in this way? Have you made enemies of the gods? Have you misused your prophetic skill? We want to help you, especially since we seem to be destined to be your saviors. But clearly the gods are punishing you, and we do not want to go against their will. We will not stop the Harpies unless you take an oath that if we do stop the Harpies we will not make enemies of the gods."

The blind old man raised his eyes and said, "Do not be afraid of incurring the wrath of the gods. I swear by Apollo, who gave me my prophetic insight, and by my own fate, and by my own blindness, and by all the gods and monsters in the Land of the Dead that you will not incur the wrath of the gods by helping me. Zeus has told me that you are fated to help me."

Zetes and Calaïs were now eager to help Phineus. The younger Argonauts prepared a meal for the blind old man — this food would be the last that the Harpies would snatch from him. Zetes and Calaïs stood beside Phineus and waited for the Harpies, who appeared as soon as Phineus touched the food. The younger Argonauts had watched for the Harpies and shouted as soon as they saw them, but the Harpies devoured the food before Zetes and Calaïs could stop them.

The Harpies flew away, and Zetes and Calaïs, who had winged feet that they had inherited from their father, the North Wind, flew after them with swords in their hands. The Harpies flew quickly and would have disappeared from sight, but Zeus gave Zetes and Calaïs speed, and they nearly caught up with the Harpies. Zetes and Calaïs managed to touch the Harpies but not harm them. They were like hounds chasing a goat or deer. The hounds try to bite their fast-fleeing prey, but the hounds' teeth bite only air. Still, Zetes and Calaïs would have caught up with and inflicted damage on the Harpies except that Iris, the messenger-goddess who is the rainbow, stopped them.

Iris said to Zetes and Calaïs, "Stop! You are not permitted to harm the Harpies. You are not permitted to attack the Harpies with your swords. Zeus has plans for the Harpies; they are his hounds. Just as hounds pursue and torment prey at the command of their masters, so the Harpies pursue and torment prey at the command of Zeus. However, I will swear to you that the Harpies will no longer torment Phineus."

Iris swore by the waters of the infernal river Styx — an inviolable oath — that the Harpies would no longer torment Phineus. This, she knew, was the working of Fate. Happy, Zetes and Calaïs turned around and flew back to Phineus and the Argonauts. Because of this, the islands underneath the place where Zetes and Calaïs turned around are now known as the Strophades, or the Turning Islands. Iris flew to Mount Olympus, and the Harpies flew to a cave in Mount Dicte on the island of Crete.

The other Argonauts washed Phineus. Then they selected the best of the sheep they had gotten when they raided the flocks of the Bebryces after the death of Amycus. They sacrificed the sheep and then prepared a feast. The Harpies stayed away, and Phineus finally ate his fill of good food — it was as if a good dream had finally come true. Everyone stayed awake all night as they waited for the return of Zetes and Calaïs.

As they waited, Phineus told them what to expect as they journeyed the rest of the way to Colchis on the eastern shore of the Black Sea. He said, "I cannot tell you all the details of the rest of your journey; the gods will permit me to reveal only part of what they have planned. Long ago, I revealed all that Zeus had planned, with the result that he sent the Harpies to punish me. Zeus wants prophecy to be incomplete. He does not want mortals to know everything.

"When you leave here, you will face the challenge of the Clashing Rocks, which are also known as the Symplegades. These rocks are not attached to the bottom of the sea, and so they crash against each other and destroy anything in between them. I do not believe that anyone has ever safely made his way between the rocks, but here is a plan that may succeed. Take a dove with you on the *Argo*, and release it when you come to the Clashing Rocks. Watch the dove. If the dove succeeds in flying between the rocks and safely reaches the other side, then follow the path of the dove as quickly as you can. Row hard and quickly. Rowing will keep you safe — you can pray later.

"But if the dove is killed as she tries to fly between the Clashing Rocks, then turn the *Argo* around and go back to your homes. Do not waste your lives. The gods will be showing you not to make the attempt. The gods will be showing you that you, too, shall die if you attempt to sail between the Clashing Rocks. Indeed, you would die even if the *Argo* were made of iron. Take advice from me, even if you think the gods hate me. Their hatred of me is not as great as you may think.

"If you succeed in sailing between the Clashing Rocks into the Black Sea, sail on with the land of the Bithynians on your right until you can beach the *Argo* on the shore of the Mariandyni people. Nearby is a path that leads to the Land of the Dead, and above this path is the mountain named Acherusias, where the waters of Acheron gush and pour into the sea.

"Continue sailing. You will see many lands, and many peoples. You will see the Mossynoeci, who live in wooden houses. They call their homes *mossynes*, and their name for themselves they have taken from their name for their homes.

"After you have passed the Mossynoeci, you will beach your ship on an island — the island of Ares. But before you beach your ship, you must find a way to drive off the very many birds that live there and do not care about mortal men. On this island, two Queens of the Amazons, Otrere and Antiope, built a stone shrine to Ares, god of war, as they prepared for war.

"Stay for a while on this island. You will find help there — help that will come from the sea. I could tell you more, but I must not out of deference to Zeus, who does not want me to reveal all of the future.

"Continue sailing until you reach the end of the Black Sea. You will see the river Phasis. Steer the *Argo* into its mouth, and you will see Aea, the city of King Aeetes. In the grove of Ares is the Golden Fleece. It is spread on an oak tree that is guarded by a huge snake that never sleeps."

Some of what Phineus told the Argonauts made them unhappy and dismayed. They were quiet for a while, and then Jason said, "You have given us much useful information, including telling us what to do when we reach the Clashing Rocks. I have other questions. Will we make it safely home again? What can I do to make that happen? Crossing all this water again will be difficult. After all, the Argonauts and I are mostly inexperienced sailors, and the city of King Aeetes is very far away from Greece."

Phineus replied, "Once you make it safely past the Clashing Rocks, you need not fear. Be aware that you will return home by a route different from the one that you took when you left Thessaly. Also be aware that the gods will help you and that you will have guides when you most need them. Remember that the goddess Aphrodite will be a most valuable ally for you. Whether your quest will be successful relies on her. Ask me no more questions."

Zetes and Calaïs arrived, and everyone rose and greeted them. Zetes, panting from the effort that he and his brother had made when pursuing the Harpies and then returning to the Argonauts, told them of the adventure and of how the goddess Iris had saved the Harpies, and of how the Harpies had flown to a cave in Mount Dicte on the island of Crete. Everyone, including Phineus, enjoyed the story.

Jason said to Phineus, "A god did care for you. The god brought us here so that Zetes and Calaïs could chase the Harpies and allow you to eat good food again. Perhaps the god shall make you see again. That would make me happy — as happy as I will be if I safely return home again."

The old man sadly said, "Sight shall not return to my ruined eyes. My eyes shall not be cured. Instead, I pray that I shall die soon. I have lived a long life, and I have lived too long. When I die, I shall find happiness."

Phineus and Jason continued to talk until dawn and visitors arrived. Each morning, visitors came to the house of Phineus to bring him food. Phineus had always treated both the rich and the poor with respect. He had used his prophetic ability to help those around him. Often, he had used his prophetic ability to prevent evil and disaster. The people respected him and brought him food.

Phineus' best friend was Paraebius, who was happy that so many strangers had come to see Phineus, who had told him that a band of strangers would arrive and free him from torment by the Harpies.

Phineus answered the questions of his visitors, using his prophetic knowledge to help them, and then he sent everyone away except for Jason and the Argonauts and Paraebius. Later, he asked Paraebius to leave and bring back sheep for sacrifice.

After Paraebius had left, Phineus gently said, "Paraebius is very grateful for a kindness I did for him. He sometimes comes here for guidance, as he did back when he had a hard time getting enough food to eat, despite all his hard work. I discovered what was happening to him. He was paying for a sin that his father had committed. His father had been cutting wood, and a Hamadryad — a female nature divinity who lives in a tree — begged him to spare the tree that she lived in and that had been her home for many years. She wept as she begged him to spare the tree — a Hamadryad dies when the tree she lives in dies. But Paraebius' father refused, and as he cut down the tree, the Hamadryad cursed him and his progeny. Paraebius came to me for help, and once I realized why he was suffering, I advised him to build an altar to the Hamadryad and to sacrifice to her and pray to her spirit to release him from the curse that she had put on his father and his father's progeny. He did that, and he was released from the curse, and his life improved. Paraebius thereafter became my best friend, and he seeks always to care for me. In fact, he is so determined to care for me that often I find it difficult to find a way to convince him to leave my house."

Paraebius came back, bringing with him two sheep to sacrifice. At Phineus' request, Jason, Zetes, and Calaïs sacrificed the sheep and prayed to Apollo. The younger Argonauts then prepared the meal. All ate, and then they slept. Some of the Argonauts slept by the ships, and some slept in the house of Phineus.

In the morning, the Etesian Winds, which are also known as the Annual Winds, were blowing. Zeus caused these winds to blow because of a descendant of a virgin shepherdess named Cyrene. Apollo saw her, desired her, and carried her off to Libya, where she bore Apollo a son named Aristaeus. Apollo took Aristaeus and gave him to the Centaur Chiron to raise. He also turned Cyrene into a long-lived nymph. After Aristaeus grew to maturity, he married a bride whom the Muses brought to him. He learned the arts of prophecy and of healing from the Muses, who also made him a shepherd. Aristaeus eventually travelled to a land where the heat was unbearable during the days that Sirius, which is also known as the Dog Star because it is the brightest star in the constellation called *Canis Major* or the Great Dog, shines brightest. During the dog days of summer, the weather grows hot and Sirius brightly shines. Aristaeus built an altar to Zeus and sacrificed both to Zeus and to Sirius. Zeus acknowledged the sacrifices by causing the Etesian Winds to blow for forty days each year during the hottest part of the summer.

Every day people brought gifts to the Argonauts because they knew that the gifts would please Phineus. In taking leave of Phineus, the Argonauts built an altar to the twelve blessed Olympian gods — Aphrodite, Apollo, Ares, Artemis, Athena, Demeter, Hephaestus, Hera, Hermes, Hestia, Poseidon, and Zeus — near his house. They then boarded the *Argo*, being careful to take a dove with them. Euphemus, the fastest man in the world — so fast that he could even run on water — carried the trembling, frightened dove.

The goddess Athena knew that the Argonauts were departing. She wanted to watch over the *Argo*, and so she stood on a cloud and rode it down to the sea and then to the coast. A traveller can visit his home in his mind — the traveller's thought quickly takes him to his home. As quickly as that did Athena move from the sky to the sea to the coast.

The *Argo* sailed into the narrowest part of the straits, and cliffs loomed above the ship on the right and the left. The undercurrent grew more powerful as the *Argo* approached the dangerous Clashing Rocks. The Argonauts could hear the rocks colliding against each other and sending water spraying into the air.

Euphemus released the dove, and the Argonauts watched it as it flew toward the Clashing Rocks and passed through them. The rocks clashed together and cut off the tips of the dove's tail feathers, but the dove lived.

The *Argo* was spun around in the white water, but the Argonauts started rowing, following the instructions of Tiphys, their pilot. The Clashing Rocks parted, and waves thrust the *Argo* between the separating rocks.

The rocks towered above the *Argo*, and the Argonauts were afraid that the rocks would clash together and sink the *Argo*. A huge wave seemed about to swamp the *Argo*, but Tiphys maneuvered the ship so that it survived the wave.

But another wave arose and put the *Argo* exactly in the spot where the Clashing Rocks hit when they came together.

This was why Athena was watching. The Argonauts needed help, and she helped them. With one hand she held on to one of the Clashing Rocks, and with her other hand she pushed the *Argo* through the Clashing Rocks to safety. The Clashing Rocks came together and broke off the tip of the *Argo*'s stern, but the *Argo* passed safely between the Clashing Rocks and into the Black Sea.

From this time forward, the Clashing Rocks were rooted to the bottom of the sea, for the gods had decided that should happen after humans had safely sailed through the Clashing Rocks.

The Argonauts had been afraid of dying, but now they were relieved and happy as they looked at the blue sky and the calm sea. They had experienced incredible danger and had survived.

Tiphys said, "We and the *Argo* have survived. I think that we can thank the goddess Athena for that. Athena helped build the *Argo*, and she gave the ship strength. The Clashing Rocks were not destined to crush the *Argo*. And now, Jason, we have survived the worst danger we will face. From the prophet Phineus we learned that once we were safely past the Clashing Rocks, we need no longer fear disaster. The gods will help us, and we will have guides when we most need them. We will face obstacles, but we will be able to overcome them."

Tiphys continued to steer the *Argo*, and Jason tested him and the other Argonauts, saying, "You are trying to give me comfort, but I know that I was wrong to undertake this quest. King Pelias wants me to get the Golden Fleece, but I should have told him that I would not make the attempt, even though I know that he would have killed me if I had stayed in the city of Iolcus. Now I am on the *Argo*, and I am filled with fear. We must cross a dangerous sea, and the natives here are sure to be our enemies. Ever since we began our journey, I have worried, and each night I cannot sleep because of my fear. You speak comforting words, Tiphys, but you have only yourself to worry about. I must worry about the safety of everybody on board the *Argo*. I worry about how I am to get all of you safely back home."

Tiphys and the other Argonauts passed the test. They remained positive and eager to continue the quest. They reassured Jason, who said to them, "You have much courage, and you make me confident that we will succeed in our quest. With you by my side, I think that I could enter the Land of the Dead and safely return. And now that we have survived the Clashing Rocks, we should not have to endure another such great danger as long as we follow the route that Phineus told us to take."

The Argonauts rowed and came to the mouth of the river Phyllis, where Phrixus had flown on the back of the golden ram and had stayed for a while as a guest of Dipsacus. The Argonauts could see Dipsacus' shrine from the *Argo* as they rowed past.

The Argonauts rowed all day and all night. They worked as hard as oxen do when pulling a plow. Sweat streamed down their bodies, and their breath was hot when they heavily exhaled.

Just before dawn, Jason and the Argonauts pulled into the harbor of the island named Thynias. They were exhausted and needed to rest. Here they saw the god Apollo as he journeyed from the country of Lycia to the northern lands and peoples. His hair was golden, he carried a silver bow in his left hand, and on his back was a quiver full of arrows. Each time he stepped on the island, it quaked. Jason and the Argonauts were awed and would not look Apollo in the eyes. They bowed their heads as Apollo walked by them and then flew into the air to continue his journey.

Orpheus said to Jason and the other Argonauts, "Let us dedicate this island to Apollo. In particular, we should dedicate it to Apollo of the Dawn because we saw Apollo at dawn. Let us build an altar on this beach and sacrifice to Apollo of the Dawn. If Apollo allows us to return to Thrace safely, we will sacrifice again to Apollo — we will burn for him the thighs of goats. Now, let us offer to Apollo the best of what we have. We shall offer him libations and burnt offerings. We shall also pray to Apollo and ask for his help."

The Argonauts followed the advice of Orpheus. While some Argonauts built the altar on the beach, other Argonauts went hunting, hoping to find a deer or a wild goat to sacrifice to Apollo of the Dawn. The hunt was successful, and the Argonauts sacrificed the animals and burnt the thighs, wrapped in fat, for Apollo.

As the thighs were burning, the Argonauts danced and sang, giving praise to Apollo. Orpheus played his lyre, and he sang a poem about the young, beardless Apollo, who shot arrows and killed the Python, a serpent, at Delphi, which is located on a spur of Mount Parnassus, and then made Delphi the site of his own oracle. Orpheus then sang, "Show us mercy and help us, Apollo. May you be proud of your long hair forever — hair that your mother, Leto, strokes with her hands."

After singing and dancing for Apollo, the Argonauts poured libations for the god. They then swore to each other to stand together and help each other forever. The Argonauts then built a temple to Harmonia, the goddess of harmony, to celebrate their concord — their agreement among people.

At dawn of the third day, a favorable wind blew, and so Jason and the Argonauts set sail. They sailed all day, but at night the wind died, and so at dawn they landed on the shore of the Mariandyni people. Here was the mountain named Acherusia, where the waters of Acheron gush and pour into the sea. A cavern with a passage leading down to the Land of the Dead is found in the mountain, and from the passage comes cold air that frosts everything until the noon Sun melts the frost. The Cave of Hades is never silent because the sound of the sea reaches it and because the cold air coming from it makes the leaves outside the cave rustle. Although the Acheron is one of the rivers found in the Land of the Dead, the harbor it pours into is known as the Sailors' Savior. Some sailors faced a storm at sea, but they found refuge in this harbor.

Lycus, the King of the Mariandyni people, welcomed Jason and the Argonauts. News of the killing of Amycus, the King of the Bebryces, had come to the Mariandyni people. The Bebryces were their enemy, and they were happy that Polydeuces had killed Amycus in the boxing match. King Lycus and the Mariandyni people treated Polydeuces like a god.

The Mariandyni people took Jason and the Argonauts to their city, and all feasted and talked. Jason told King Lycus about each of the Argonauts, giving him their names and histories. He told King Lycus about their quest for the Golden Fleece, about their adventures on the island of Lemnos and in other lands, about how they left Heracles behind, about the Harpies, about Phineus' advice to the Argonauts, about sailing through the Clashing Rocks, and about seeing the god Apollo.

King Lycus enjoyed Jason's stories, but he lamented that Jason and the Argonauts had left behind Heracles: "You lost a strong and brave man when you left Heracles behind. It's a pity that he could not have sailed with you to Colchis. I myself have seen Heracles. He came to my father's palace after completing one of his labors. Eurystheus had ordered Heracles to get the war-belt of Hippolyta, the queen of the Amazons, war-like women who learn the skills of war such as archery from birth. Heracles sailed with other warriors to the Amazons, and he ambushed and captured Melanippe, Queen Hippolyta's sister. Hippolyta gave up her war-belt as ransom for her sister. However, Hera caused trouble. She told the Amazons that Heracles was planning to kidnap Hippolyta, and the Amazons attacked Heracles, who sailed away with Hippolyta's war-belt. When Heracles came to my father's palace, I was still very young. I had only down on my cheeks.

"Heracles, of course, is the best boxer ever. Our enemies killed Priolas, my brother, whom my people still mourn. Heracles attended the funeral. He boxed our champion boxer, Titias, and he knocked out all of Titias' teeth.

"Heracles helped my father. After the funeral games for Priolas, Heracles fought and defeated all of our enemies. Heracles fought so fiercely that some of our enemies surrendered because they did not want to fight Heracles.

"But Heracles has been away for a long time now, and so our former enemies are again harrying us. They have stolen much of our land. However, you and Polydeuces have made them pay. I have to believe that the gods' plan was for you to come here and for Polydeuces to kill King Amycus. It could not be by accident that on the very day that Amycus died I was making war on his people and attacking his villages and vineyards.

"I want to reward you. That is how it should be when the strong help the weak. I will send Dascylus, my son, with you on your quest. With him aboard, the peoples you see during your voyage to Colchis will know that you are friendly and will not attack you.

"I will also build a temple to Polydeuces and Castor on a height so that sailors at sea will look at and admire it. I will regard Polydeuces and Castor as gods, and I will dedicate land to them."

Jason and the Argonauts and King Lycus and the Mariandyni people celebrated and feasted all day, and the next morning the Argonauts returned to the *Argo*, which King Lycus had loaded with gifts. Dascylus, the son of King Lycus, went to the shore to sail away with the Argonauts.

But now Idmon, the man of prophecy, met his fate. Despite his skill in reading the signs of birds, death came for him. A huge boar with white tusks cooled himself in a marsh by a river. The boar was so dangerous that even the water-nymphs were afraid of it. As Idmon was walking along the muddy bank of the river, the boar attacked him and gored his thigh, breaking the bone and severing the sinews. Idmon screamed and fell. The Argonauts ran to help him, and Peleus, the father of Achilles, threw his javelin at the boar but missed. The boar attacked, and Idas, who lacked tact but did not lack strength and courage, impaled it with a spear. They left the boar behind and carried Idmon to the *Argo*, where he died with his friends around him.

For three days, all mourned the death of Idmon, and on the fourth day they buried him. Jason and the Argonauts and King Lycus and the Mariandyni people all participated in the funeral rites. They sacrificed many sheep, and they built a burial mound for the dead hero. The burial mound bears as a monument a ship's roller made from a wild olive tree.

Apollo commanded some people to build a town around the burial mound and to show honor to Idmon. These people, however, prefer to show honor to Agamestor, their own hero, than to Idmon.

A second hero died, and the Argonauts built his burial mound close by the burial mound of Idmon. The pilot of the *Argo*, Tiphys, suffered a brief illness after the funeral of Idmon, and he died of the illness.

The grief of Jason and the Argonauts at burying two friends was so great that they fell into a depression and would not eat or drink but instead lay on the ground by the sea. They resembled stone statues more than living human beings. They did not speak. They did not hope to return home.

The goddess Hera inspired Ancaeus, son of Poseidon, to bring the Argonauts out of their depression and give them hope. Like Tiphys, he had learned the skills of steering a ship.

Ancaeus said to Peleus, father of Achilles, "Why have we given up our quest? Why do we stay here? Jason made me an Argonaut not because of my fighting ability, but because of my seamanship. We have lost Tiphys, the pilot of the *Argo*, but I also can steer a ship. And not just me, but other Argonauts have the ability to be a competent pilot. Others and I know the sea and ships, and we would not steer the *Argo* into danger. Talk to the Argonauts. Remind them of our quest."

Peleus stood up and said, "Argonauts, let us now stop grieving. Two of us have died, including our pilot, but that was their fate. We have our own fates. Some of us Argonauts know the sea and ships. We can choose a new pilot. Let us continue our quest without delay. Let us get up, and let us sail."

Jason, still depressed, said, "Peleus, which men are you talking about? Who can serve as the pilot of the *Argo*? The other Argonauts are even more depressed than I am. I see nothing ahead for us except the same fate that befell Idmon and Tiphys: death. I do not think that we shall ever reach Colchis, the land of King Aeetes, nor do I think that we shall ever return to the city of Iolcus in Thessaly. No. We shall grow old here. We shall die here. We shall have accomplished nothing with our lives."

Ancaeus volunteered to serve as pilot of the *Argo*. So did Erginus, a son of Poseidon. So did Nauplius, who was descended from King Danaus. So did Euphemus, the fastest man in the world — he was so fast that he could run on water.

From these four candidates to be the pilot of the *Argo*, the Argonauts elected Ancaeus.

On the twelfth day since landing in a harbor of King Lycus and the Mariandyni people, a favorable wind blew and the Argonauts rowed out of the harbor and sailed away.

Sailing, they saw the mouth of the River Callichorus. Here the god Dionysus, god of wine and ecstasy, had stopped for a while as he traveled from India to Thebes. He had lived in a cave, and he taught his rituals to the people he found, and they danced for him.

Continuing to sail, the Argonauts saw the tomb of Sthenelus, who had journeyed to the land of the Amazons with Heracles to get the war-belt of Hippolyta, the Amazonian Queen. Wounded by an arrow, he died here and his mourners raised a burial mound for him. In the Land of the Dead, Sthenelus asked Persephone, Queen of the Dead, for permission to see the Argonauts, a wish that she granted.

The Argonauts saw the ghost of Sthenelus, who was wearing the armor, including a four-horned helmet, that he had worn as a warrior. The ghost stood on his burial mound, watched the Argonauts briefly, and then sank down again to the Land of the Dead. Mopsus, whom Apollo had trained in the arts of divination, told the Argonauts to land and pour libations to honor the ghost of Sthenelus. The Argonauts landed and poured libations to the ghost. They also sacrificed sheep. Further away, they built an altar to honor Apollo and burned the thighbones of the sheep as an offering to the god. Orpheus also made an offering to Apollo: a lyre. For this reason, the region is now called Lyra.

Jason and the Argonauts set sail in a strong wind. It moved quickly, like an eagle gliding in a breeze that swiftly carries it. They sailed by the Parthenius River, in which the virgin goddess Artemis is known to bathe after a hunt. After refreshing herself, she ascends to Olympus. The *Argo* sailed both day and night.

Jason and the Argonauts next landed on the coast of Assyria, where Zeus had carried Sinope. He had wanted to have sex with her, but she made him promise by the Styx River — an inviolable oath — to grant one wish to her. Zeus swore the oath, thinking that after granting the wish he could sleep with her, but Sinope outwitted him: She wished to keep her virginity. Not wanting anyone to know that he had been outwitted, Zeus kept the story quiet, with the result that Sinope was able to use the same trick on Apollo and on the god of the Halys River. An intelligent woman who was devoted to virginity, Sinope used other tricks to keep mortal men from sleeping with her. Throughout her life, she remained a virgin.

On the coast of Assyria were living three former companions of Heracles: Deileon, Autolycus, and Phlogius. They were brothers: sons of Deimachus. They had accompanied Heracles when he journeyed to the land of the Amazons to get the war-belt of Hippolyta, Queen of the Amazons. Unfortunately, they had become separated from Heracles and so remained in this land. When they saw the Argonauts land on shore, they met them and asked to be taken aboard the *Argo*, a request that the Argonauts readily granted. The Argonauts stayed on the shore for only a brief time because the wind was favorable, and then they set sail with the three new heroes on board.

That same day, they came to the harbor of the Amazons. Here Heracles had ambushed and captured Melanippe, the sister of Hippolyta. In ransom for Melanippe, Hippolyta gave Heracles her war-belt.

Jason and the Argonauts landed at the mouth of the Thermodon River, which has many branches. Here the Argonauts and the Amazons could have fought, and it would have been a bloody fight. The Amazons are not gentle women; they are brutal. The Amazons are descended from Ares, god of war, who had sex with the nymph Harmonia — she bore the same name as the goddess of harmony. She bore him girls who love war. The Amazons live in three areas with three leaders. The Themiscyreans, who have Hippolyta as their leader, live on the beach. The other Amazons — the Lycastians and the javelin-throwing Chadesians — live in other areas.

No fight occurred because Zeus sent a favorable wind, and again the *Argo* set sail — just in time because the Amazons were arming for battle.

The next day they landed at sunset in the land of the Chalybes, who are miners, not farmers. They mine iron and sell it for money to buy food and other necessities. They work hard, and they work every day in a land without holidays.

The Argonauts set sail and passed by the land of the Tibareni, where when women gave birth, their husbands lay in bed and groaned. The women giving birth tend to their husbands and feed them and prepare baths for them.

Again the Argonauts set sail and saw a strange people: the Mossynoeci, who live in wooden houses that they call *mossynes*. These people have incorrect ideas about what is right and wrong. The things that good people do in public, the Mossynoeci do in private. The things that good people do in private, the Mossynoeci do in public. They are like pigs. They even have promiscuous sex in public. They have a king, and the king dispenses justice, but if his subjects disagree with one of the king's decisions, they lock him up and do not feed or release him until the following day.

The Argonauts set sail and saw a strange sight: the island of Ares, god of war. Here are dangerous birds whose feathers are weapons. One of the war-god's birds flew over the *Argo* and released a pointed feather. The feather's point speared the shoulder of Oileus, the father of Little Ajax, who would be a Greek hero in the Trojan War. Injured, Oileus dropped his oar. His companion, Eribotes, who rowed in the seat next to him, tended the wound. He pulled out the feather, removed Oileus' war-belt, and bandaged the wound.

Another bird of Ares came flying over the *Argo*, but this time the Argonauts realized the danger they were in. Clytius, son of the archer Eurytus, shot an arrow into the bird, which fell beside the *Argo*.

Amphidamas said to the Argonauts, "We know that we are close to the island of Ares because these are his birds. But we need to think what to do. Phineus told us to land here because we would find help here. But he also told us to find a way to drive away these birds. I do not think that our bows and arrows will be enough to keep us from danger.

"Heracles himself had trouble with birds. The Stymphalian birds killed human beings, and they lived in a marshy part of the Stymphalian Lake.

Heracles drove away the birds with noise. He made a loud racket, and the birds were afraid and flew away. I myself witnessed this.

"Let us make a noise like Heracles did. We can arm ourselves and put on our helmets, and then half of us can row while the other half of us serve as guards. As needed, we can take turns rowing and guarding. The guards can hold their shields overhead, locking the shields together like tiles on the roof of a house. The shields will create a protective tortoise shell over our heads. All of us can shout and make noise that will scare away the birds of Ares. When we land on the island, we can make additional noise by banging on our shields with our swords."

Jason and the Argonauts agreed with Amphidamas' plan. They put on their helmets, and half of the Argonauts rowed while the other half used their shields to form what looked like a tortoise shell above their heads. All shouted, making a noise similar to that of two armies coming together and fighting. They saw no birds of Ares — not yet. But when they landed on the island of Ares and banged on their shields with their swords, they saw thousands of Ares' birds rise into the air and drop pointed feathers on them before they flew far away. The pointed feathers did no damage. The Argonauts' tortoise shell protected them. They were like people in a house with a solidly constructed roof that withstands hailstones.

Phineus had made a prophecy: Jason and the Argonauts would find help here.

Phineus' prophecy was true. The day after the *Argo* landed on the island of Ares, four sons of Phrixus were shipwrecked there because of a storm that rose that night. The four sons of Phrixus had left the city of King Aeetes and were sailing to the city of Orchomenus in Boeotia to recover the possessions of their father, who had told them to do this. These possessions had belonged to Athamas, Phrixus' father, and when Athamas died, the possessions were supposed to be passed down to Phrixus. But Zeus sent the North Wind to stop them. At first, the North Wind blew very softly, but then at night it roared and created huge waves that battered their ship into pieces. The four sons of Phrixus held onto a huge wooden beam as they were battered by waves and wind. But they made their way to the island of Ares, and morning came and the storm stopped.

As the Sun rose, the four sons of Phrixus saw the Argonauts and approached them. One of the sons had the same name as the builder of the *Argo*. This son, Argus, spoke first. "We ask you, whoever you are, to help us. Our ship has sunk, and we barely made it alive to shore. While we were in the stormy sea, we lost much of the clothing we were wearing, and so we ask you for clothing we can use to cover our nakedness. We ask that you respect Zeus, the god of hospitality, by helping us. We are suppliants, and Zeus is the god of suppliants."

Jason realized that another of the prophecies of Phineus was coming true: Here was the help that Phineus had prophesied.

Jason said to the four sons of Phrixus, "We are happy to give you clothing and whatever else you need. But please tell us who you are."

Argus replied, "No doubt you have already heard the story of Phrixus, who rode a winged ram whose fleece Hermes had made golden. Phrixus rode the ram through the air to Colchis, the land of King Aeetes on the east coast of the Black Sea. The Golden Fleece of the ram still exists; it is displayed on an oak tree. After the ram had carried Phrixus to safety, the ram itself told Phrixus to sacrifice it to Zeus, the god who protects refugees. King Aeetes welcomed Phrixus and treated him well, even giving his daughter Chalciope in marriage to Phrixus without requiring any payment from him. Phrixus and Chalciope were the parents of us four — we are brothers. Phrixus died of old age in the palace of King Aeetes, and as our father wanted, we began a journey to the city of Orchomenus to take over the estate of Athamas, our grandfather. His estate had been intended to pass on to Phrixus and then to us. However, during our voyage a storm arose and sank our ship. My name is Argus, and the names of my three brothers are Cytissorus, Phrontis, and Melas."

Jason and the Argonauts were both amazed and happy to find out who the four men were.

Jason said, "You four men and I are related by blood. Your grandfather, Athamas, and my grandfather, Cretheus, were brothers. Phrixus traveled to the city of King Aeetes, and I am doing the same. Later, we will talk more. First let me attend to your needs and provide you with clothing. The gods must have deliberately brought me here to help you."

The four sons of Phrixus put on clothing brought from the *Argo*, and everyone made their way to the temple and sacrificed sheep to Ares on an outside altar. Ares' temple had no roof, and inside it was a sacred black rock. The Amazons came occasionally to the temple to pray to the black rock. They sacrificed neither sheep nor oxen; instead, they sacrificed horses, of which they had large herds.

After the animals had been sacrificed and everyone had eaten, Jason stood up and said to the four sons of Phrixus, "Zeus sees all and rewards men who properly worship him. A hateful stepmother could have murdered Phrixus, but Zeus saved his life and made him safe in a foreign land. You four sons of Phrixus could have perished in the storm at sea, but now you are safe and you have a choice: on the *Argo*, you can sail with us either to the city of King Aeetes or to the city of Orchomenus. The *Argo* is not an ordinary ship. The goddess Athena built the *Argo* with wood that she herself cut with her bronze ax on Mount Pelion. With Athena's help, the *Argo* sailed safely through the Clashing Rocks — rocks that your own ship never reached. I hope that you will choose to go with us to the city of King Aeetes. We are going to acquire the Golden Fleece and take it back with us when we return home. Zeus was angry at the attempted murder of Phrixus, and we intend to appease Zeus with the Golden Fleece. That is our quest."

Jason spoke well, but the four sons of Phrixus were troubled by what he said. Getting the Golden Fleece from King Aeetes would be difficult. He had treated Phrixus kindly, but he was not always a kind man.

Argus, who did not want to be a part of the quest to acquire the Golden Fleece, said to Jason, "We will help you in any way we can when trouble arises, but this quest of yours is dangerous. King Aeetes can be a formidable enemy. He says that he is the son of Helios, he has many warriors, and he has mighty muscles and a terrifying voice.

"To get the Golden Fleece without the permission and help of King Aeetes will be dangerous and difficult. A snake that never sleeps and cannot die guards the Golden Fleece. The goddess Earth gave birth to the snake beside the rock where the large and fearsome monster Typhaon fought Zeus and was defeated. Zeus hit Typhaon with a thunderbolt, and Typhaon bled as he traveled to the land of Nysa, where he is today, lying beneath the water of Lake Serbonis."

Argus' words troubled many of the Argonauts, but Peleus replied to Argus, "Do not be more wary than you ought to be. We are warriors, not feeble men. If we have to fight the men of King Aeetes, we will. We know as much about war as he does, and some of us are also the sons of gods. If he will not willingly give us the Golden Fleece, his warriors will not stop us from taking it from him."

More debate took place, and then all slept. At dawn, a favorable wind blew, and all went on board the *Argo* and sailed and quickly left behind the island of Ares.

When night fell, they passed the island of Philyra, where Uranus deceived his wife, Rhea, and had sex with Philyra, the daughter of Ocean. Rhea discovered them having sex together. In an attempt to deceive Rhea, Cronus had transformed himself into a stallion. He galloped away. Because of Cronus' transformation, Philyra gave birth to the Centaur Chiron, who was half horse and half god.

The *Argo* continued its journey, and Jason and the Argonauts saw Mount Caucasus, where Zeus had chained all the limbs of Prometheus, who had stolen fire and taught Humankind to master it. To punish Prometheus further, each day Zeus sent an eagle to devour his liver, which grew back each night so the eagle could devour it again the following day. Jason and the Argonauts saw the eagle flying to Prometheus. This eagle was different from other eagles. It did not flap its wings; instead, it used the feathers of each wing like oars as it rowed through the air. After the eagle flew out of sight, they heard Prometheus screaming. After the eagle finished its meal, Jason and the Argonauts saw the eagle fly back to its home.

And now the *Argo* reached its destination: the land of Colchis on the east coast of the Black Sea. Jason and the Argonauts lowered the sail and stored it, and they took down the mast. They rowed into a river. On one side was Mount Caucasus and Aea, the major city of Colchis. On their other side was the field of Ares; this was where the huge snake guarded the Golden Fleece in a grove that was sacred to the god of war.

Jason poured libations of pure wine into the river as he prayed to gods and the spirits of heroes to give the Argonauts and him help.

Bearskin-wearing Ancaeus said, "Now we must take thought about how best to achieve our quest. Should we approach King Aeetes with fair words, or should we take a different approach toward achieving our goal?"

Jason did not answer immediately. He followed the advice of Argus, son of Phrixus, and told the Argonauts to row into the marshes and anchor the *Argo* there. They then waited for dawn.

Chapter 3: Jason, Medea, and the Dragon's Teeth

Hera and Athena were watching Jason and the Argonauts from Mount Olympus. They left Zeus and the other gods and talked privately.

Hera said to Athena, "Tell me what you think we ought to do. Can you think of a trick that will get the Golden Fleece into Jason's hands? Or should we let Jason speak persuasively to King Aeetes, who we know will not want to give up the Golden Fleece? We ought, I think, to consider all the possible ways in which Jason may acquire the Golden Fleece."

Athena replied, "You are asking the questions that I have been thinking about. Unfortunately, I have not yet thought up a good plan for Jason to follow."

The two goddesses stared down at the floor as they thought.

Hera then said, "Let us speak to Aphrodite. Her son has arrows that cause people to fall in love. Perhaps she can persuade him to shoot an arrow into the heart of Medea, the daughter of King Aeetes, and cause her to fall in love with Jason. Medea knows many spells, but not even she can resist the powers of the arrows of the immortal son of Aphrodite."

Athena, a virgin goddess, replied, "I have never been the victim of any of her son's arrows, and I know nothing of love charms. In fact, I know nothing of the sexual ways of males and females. I was not even born by way of a mother's birth canal. As you know, Zeus heard a prophecy that my mother's first child would be a daughter, but her second child would be a son who would overthrow his father. Therefore, he swallowed my mother, whose name was Metis. After a while, Zeus got a headache. Hephaestus knew what to do: he split Zeus' head with an ax, and I sprang out of Zeus' head, fully grown and fully armed. Zeus, being immortal, healed quickly. Let us do as you wish, Hera. When we meet Aphrodite, you do the talking."

They went to the palace of Aphrodite. When Hephaestus, the lame blacksmith god, married her, he built this palace. Hera and Athena went into the courtyard and onto the veranda outside the bedroom where Hephaestus and Aphrodite slept together. Hephaestus had already left to go to his workshop on a floating island. Aphrodite was still at home, combing her hair and preparing to braid it.

Aphrodite greeted Hera and Athena and invited them to sit down. She did not finish combing her hair.

Aphrodite, the goddess of sexual passion, loved laughter, and she spoke to her guests, whom she had recently defeated in a beauty contest, with a little too obvious excessive praise: "I am honored by your presence. You two are the greatest goddesses of all."

The three goddesses usually got along, although they could be rivals. When Peleus had married the sea-nymph Thetis, Eris, who is the goddess of discord, had shown up at the wedding with a golden apple inscribed "for the fairest female." Hera, Athena, and Aphrodite had each considered herself the most beautiful female, and they had competed in a beauty contest for the apple. Zeus would not judge the beauty contest because he knew that he would make two goddesses very angry at him, and so Paris, Prince of Troy, judged the beauty contest in what became known as the Judgment of Paris. Each of the three goddesses offered him a bribe to choose her, and Paris accepted the bribe of Aphrodite — who promised him the most beautiful woman in the world — and so Paris said that Aphrodite was the most beautiful of the three goddesses. The most beautiful woman in the world was Helen, who was married to Menelaus, King of Sparta. Later, Paris would travel to Sparta and run away with Helen, taking her to Troy. Menelaus and his older brother, Agamemnon, would raise an army and travel to Troy to get Helen back. Helen would become known as Helen of Troy, and the war fought over Helen would become known as the Trojan War.

Hera, all too aware of Aphrodite's fulsome praise, said, "This is no time for comedy or sarcasm. We have urgent business. Jason and the Argonauts are now on the *Argo*, which is anchored in the Phasis River in Colchis. They want to acquire the Golden Fleece — a difficult task — and we are worried about Jason in particular. I will fight for Jason, and I will protect him wherever he goes — even if he should sail into the Land of the Dead to release Ixion, who lusted for me and wanted to sleep with me, but my husband, Zeus, fooled him with a replica of me and then punished him by placing him on a fiery spinning wheel in the Land of the Dead. But I want to punish King Pelias of the city of Iolcus. That man must not be allowed to say that he insulted me without being punished for his insolence. He offers sacrifices to all of the gods — except me! For that, he must be and will be punished. In addition, I personally like Jason. I disguised myself as an old mortal woman and went down to the mortals to test their character. I wanted to know whether mortals would be generous and kind or cheap and hard-hearted. I met Jason, who had been hunting, at the mouth of the flooded Anaurus River and told him that I needed to cross it. He carried me on his back across the river. Because of that good deed, I will protect Jason. I want to punish King Pelias by helping Jason to acquire the Golden Fleece and successfully take it home. For that to happen, I need your help."

Aphrodite was briefly silent. Hera, the wife of Zeus, the king of gods and men, did not often request favors from her. Without sarcasm, she replied, "Hera, queen of goddesses, I will do whatever I can to help you. To do otherwise would be wrong. You need not give me anything in return."

Hera said, "We do not need force; we need trickery. We want you to tell your son to make Medea, the daughter of King Aeetes, fall in love with Jason. Medea knows many spells; she is a sorceress. With her help, Jason will be able to acquire the Golden Fleece and take it back to the city of Iolcus."

Aphrodite replied, "My son is difficult to control. He would obey you two sooner than he would me. My son is naughty and acts disrespectfully to me. For you two, he may display the proper manners. He ignores my wishes, and whenever I want him to do something, he does the opposite. I am tempted to break his bow and his arrows right in front of him whenever I remember how he threatened me — he told me, 'Leave me alone, or you will regret what I will do to you.' I think that he was thinking of shooting me with an arrow and making me fall in love with a disgraceful being — perhaps even a mortal."

Hera and Athena glanced at each other and smiled. In fact, Aphrodite had a mortal son, Aeneas, who would be a hero of the Trojan War. He would survive the war and go to Italy and found a city. Aeneas' father was Anchises, a mortal man with whom Aphrodite had once fallen in love.

Aphrodite saw the glance and said, "Others laugh at my troubles, but my troubles are serious. I should never refer to them — unfortunately, everyone knows about them. But I will do as you wish. I will find my son and persuade him to make Medea fall in love with Jason. I will find a way."

Hera smiled and held Aphrodite's hand and said to her, "Thank you, but please act quickly. And don't scold your boy when he annoys you. He will grow more mature."

Hera and Athena left, and Aphrodite began to search for her son. Both he and Ganymede, a mortal boy whom Zeus had kidnapped because of his great beauty, were in Zeus' orchard, playing a game with golden knucklebones. Aphrodite's immortal son, whose name was Eros, had won most of the knucklebones, and he was happy. Ganymede had only two knucklebones left, and he was unhappy. The game ended quickly — Eros now had all the knucklebones. Eros laughed as Ganymede walked away.

Aphrodite went to Eros and held his head in her hands and said, "Why are you so happy? I think you cheated — that's how you won. Ganymede is only a mortal child, but you took advantage of him.

"Listen. I want you to do me a favor. If you do it for me, I will give you something: a toy that Zeus, when he was a child, played with. His nurse, Adrestia, made this toy for him when he was living in a cave in Mount Ida on the island of Crete. Not even Hephaestus could make a better toy. Look at it. It is a perfect ball made of golden hoops cleverly stitched together so that you cannot see the stitches. When it is yours, you can throw it into the air, and it will leave a fiery trail behind it, just like a falling star does. I will give you this perfect ball only after you shoot one of your arrows into Medea's heart and make her fall in love with Jason. But you must do that immediately, or I will not give you this perfect ball."

Eros wanted the perfect ball — right now. He threw his toys on the ground, put his arms around his mother, and begged her for the ball, but she kissed his cheeks and said, "I will not give you the ball yet. First, you have to shoot an arrow into Medea's heart and make her fall in love with Jason."

Eros gathered his knucklebones and counted them and gave them to his mother for her to take care of. He got his quiver, which was leaning against a nearby tree, and slung it over his shoulder. He then picked up his bow and left Zeus' orchard. He went through the gates of Olympus and headed down to the world of the mortals with its farms and large cities and its rivers, mountains, and sea.

Jason and the Argonauts were still on board the *Argo*, which was well hidden in the marshes of the river. They talked and planned together, and Jason said, "I will tell you what I want to do, but all of us have the ability — and the duty — to point out strengths and weaknesses in plots. If you keep silent when you ought to speak — perhaps to point out a weakness in a plot — then you are endangering our quest as well as ourselves.

"I want you to stay on the *Argo* and be ready for any possible trouble. Keep your weapons by you. I myself, along with the four sons of Phrixus and two Argonauts, will go to the palace of King Aeetes and talk to him. I want to see if he will give us the Golden Fleece or if we shall have to fight him to get it. When we find out what kind of person King Aeetes is, we will be better prepared to deal with him. We will know whether we ought to fight him and his men in open battle or we ought to find a way of getting the Golden Fleece without having to fight a battle. We should not immediately fight and take away the Golden Fleece from him without at least talking to him first and trying to get the Golden Fleece without bloodshed. Persuasive speech can succeed where forceful violence fails. All of us should remember that King Aeetes treated Phrixus well when Phrixus rode the golden ram to this country to escape from his stepmother, who wanted him dead. Even an evil man can fear Zeus, the god of hospitality, and therefore the evil man can be kind to strangers."

The younger Argonauts voiced their approval of Jason's plan and none of the older Argonauts spoke against it or suggested a different plan, so Jason, the four sons of Phrixus, along with Telamon, who was the father of Great Ajax, and Augeias, a wealthy Argonaut, set out to talk to King Aeetes. Jason carried the scepter of Hermes, god of heralds, in his hand to show that he and the others were owed the rights of heralds.

Jason and the others walked to the high ground of a plain that is called Circe, where the Colchians give their dead both to the air and to the earth. They do not burn or bury the corpses of their men; instead, they wrap them in untanned oxhide and then hang them with ropes from the trees. The Colchians bury the corpses of their women.

As Jason and the others walked to King Aeetes' city, Hera spread mist throughout the city and country so that Jason and the others would not be noticed until they had reached the palace of King Aeetes. At that time, she dissolved the mist.

Jason and the others marveled at the courtyard with its wide gates and the palace with its many columns and its marble and bronze. They entered the courtyard. Nearby were four springs that Hephaestus had created. From the first spring flowed milk, from the second spring flowed wine, from the third spring flowed sweet-smelling oil, and from the fourth spring flowed water that was hot in winter and cold in summer. Such was the engineering skill of Hephaestus, who also created bronze bulls that breathed fire. A final work of art by Hephaestus was a steel plow made in one piece. Hephaestus had created the steel plow to honor Helios, who when Hephaestus sank, exhausted, on the battlefield where the gods and the giants fought, had taken him to safety in his chariot. The gods, helped by Heracles, won this fight. The giant Alcyoneus led the forces of Chaos against the gods. The fight occurred in Alcyoneus' homeland, and since Alcyoneus could not be killed in his homeland, Heracles, who was fighting on the side of the Olympian gods, picked him up and carried across the border and then killed him.

Jason and the others saw the inner court with its well-made doors and decorated galleries, and they saw many high buildings. In one high building, King Aeetes and his wife, Eidyia, who was the youngest daughter of Oceanus and Tethys, lived. In another high building lived Apsyrtus, the son whom King Aeetes had had with the nymph Asterodia before he married Eidyia, the mother of his two daughters. Apsyrtus was nicknamed Phaeton, which means the Shining One — in any group of the young men of Colchis, Apsyrtus outshone the others.

Women lived in the other buildings: servants and King Aeetes' two daughters, who were Chalciope, the widow of Phrixus, and Medea, the priestess of Hecate, goddess of witchcraft. Medea was looking for her sister now. Hera had caused Medea to stay at home, but normally Medea would have been in the temple of Hecate. When Medea saw Jason and his companions, she was startled and cried out. Chalciope and the female servants heard the cry, and they came to see why Medea had cried out.

Chalciope saw her sons with Jason, and she was filled with joy. Her four sons were also joyful, and they hugged their mother. She said to them, "So you have quickly returned! I am happy, but I suffered and worried while you were gone. Were your desires for travel and for your grandfather's estate really so important? You obeyed your dying father's wish, true, but by doing so, you brought misery to me. Is it really worthwhile to go to the city of someone named Orchomenus to claim your grandfather's estate? Is doing that really worth abandoning your mother and leaving her behind to suffer and worry?"

The final two people to enter the courtyard were King Aeetes and Queen Eidyia. They had heard Chalciope cry out with joy and so came out of their house to see what was going on. With the arrival of King Aeetes, his slaves immediately set to work to provide food and baths for the guests. Some butchered a bull, some chopped wood, and some heated water for bathing. No one wanted to be punished by King Aeetes for not working.

Eros, the son of Aphrodite, now arrived. He was like a gadfly that annoys herding animals. Now he wanted to interfere in the life of a mortal woman. Unseen by mortal humans, he took an arrow and fitted it to his bow. Taking a position at the feet of Jason, he drew the bow as far as it would bend, and he shot the arrow deep into the heart of Medea. And she fell in love with Jason.

Eros laughed and left to seek his mother and take possession of the perfect ball. Medea kept looking at Jason. A servant will start a fire in the early morning. A log smolders from the night before, and when the servant puts kindling on it, the kindling quickly catches fire and burns high. Medea burned like that fire. As she looked at Jason, her cheeks turned red, then white, then red again.

King Aeetes gave Jason and his companions hospitality. The visitors to King Aeetes' court enjoyed hot baths and then sat down for a meal with the others. After everyone had eaten, King Aeetes asked his four grandsons, the sons of his daughter Chalciope, "Why are you back in the city of Aea so quickly? Did you run into some misfortune? You went on what was supposed to be a long journey, although I do not think that you knew how long it really was. I know because I traveled that way myself long ago in the chariot of my father, Helios, god of the Sun. He took the goddess Circe — who is my sister — and me to the Western Land, where she still lives. Tell me what happened during your voyage and tell me who are these companions of yours."

Argus, the oldest of the King Aeetes' four grandsons, worried about how King Aeetes would treat Jason and the Argonauts. Argus answered, "Our ship did not last long — a storm tore it into pieces. We survived by holding onto a wooden beam and were washed onto the island of Ares. The gods looked after us. The birds that are normally on the island are dangerous, but they had been driven away by these men who are here with us. These men had landed on the island the day before. Apparently, the gods had intended for these men to help us by giving us clothing and food and safe passage home. Or perhaps it was fated. But when they heard your name and the name Phrixus, they helped us. They themselves were already sailing to your city.

"These men have a purpose in coming here. King Pelias of Iolcus sent them here on what the king believes is a hopeless quest. That king would like for these men never to return to their homes. Their quest is to acquire the Golden Fleece and return it to the city of Iolcus in Thessaly. According to King Pelias, that is the only way to expiate the evil deed of the attempt to kill my father, Phrixus, who as you know flew here on the golden ram to escape his evil stepmother, who wanted him dead. In addition, by acquiring the Golden Fleece, Jason will show that he is capable of ruling Iolcus, which King Pelias rules as usurper.

"The ship they sail on is the *Argo*, which the goddess Athena helped build. Obviously, it is a better ship than the ships of our country. My brothers and I must have gotten the worst of all Colchian ships since it fell apart so quickly. In contrast, the *Argo* provides safe sailing even in storms, and it sails well whether it is powered by winds or by oars.

"The leader of the *Argo* sailed here with the best of the men of Greece, and he sailed here a great distance, passing many lands and peoples, in the hope that you will give him the Golden Fleece. Whether you do that is up to you. He has not come here to take it by force. Instead, he is willing to pay for it by warring against your enemies, the Sauromatae, and making them weak. I have given Jason information about the Sauromatae.

"Let me introduce these men to you. This is Jason, the leader of the *Argo*. He is related to us on our father's side because he and we have grandfathers who were brothers. He is a grandson of Cretheus, and we — your four grandsons — had a grandfather named Athamas, who was the father of our father, Phrixus. Cretheus and Athamas were brothers.

"The two men with Jason are Augeias, who is a son of Helios, god of the Sun, and Telamon, son of Aeacus, who is a son of Zeus. The men who sail with Jason are illustrious: They are the sons or the grandsons of gods."

King Aeetes did not want to give up the Golden Fleece, and he grew angry as he listened to the words of Argus. He was especially angry at all four of his grandsons, whom he blamed for bringing Jason and the Argonauts to his city.

He was also angry at Jason and the Argonauts, whom he thought wanted to overthrow him and let his four grandsons assume power.

King Aeetes told his four grandsons, "Get out! Get out of my palace and out of my country! You and these men are not after the Golden Fleece — you are after my kingdom! You have eaten at my table and so you are my guests and I must treat you as guests or risk angering Zeus, the god of hospitality. But if you had not eaten at my table, I would mutilate you. I would have your tongues cut out of your mouths and have your hands cut off. I would send you out of my palace with only your feet. That would teach you not to go on voyages and plot to take my kingdom. And as for what you said about Jason's men being the sons and grandsons of god, that is a lie!"

King Aeetes, ruler of the Colchians, had the power to mutilate his guests — and relatives. Zeus, god of hospitality, had the power to do much worse — eternally — to King Aeetes.

Telamon, the grandson of Zeus, was about to shout in anger at King Aeetes, but Jason stopped him and spoke to the king diplomatically, "King Aeetes, please ignore any weapons that I and the others have. It is not our intention to make war against you. We have made a dangerous journey, and our weapons are simply for our protection and for hunting. The journey we have made has been very dangerous, and we have made it only because of our fates and because of the orders of cruel King Pelias. Help us, and we will make your name famous in Greece. In addition, we are willing to fight and conquer your enemy: the Sauromatae."

King Aeetes was still angry despite Jason's diplomatic speech. He sat quietly, trying to decide what to do. Should he kill Jason, Augeias, and Telamon and risk the anger of Zeus, the god of hospitality? Or should he challenge Jason to accomplish a task — a task that would kill him? He decided to give Jason a task that the king thought would be impossible for Jason to survive.

He said to Jason, "If you and your men can prove to me that you are worthy to have the Golden Fleece, I will give it to you. But first you have to prove that you are worthy. Therefore, you will have to accomplish something that I myself have already accomplished. On the field of Ares, I have two bulls. They breathe fire and have bronze feet. I yoke them to a plow and plow a four-acre field that I plant not with grain, but with the teeth of a huge dragon. From these seeds spring fully grown, fully armed warriors, whom I kill with my spear. All of this

I do in a single day: In the morning, I plow, and by the end of the evening, I have finished my harvesting. If you can do what I have done, then you may carry away the Golden Fleece. If you cannot do what I have done, then you cannot have the Golden Fleece — you are not worthy to have it. It takes a brave man to do what I have done, and a coward ought not to possess the Golden Fleece."

Jason looked at the floor and thought of the task that King Aeetes wanted him to perform. Jason knew that the task was dangerous and difficult to perform, and he was reluctant to try to accomplish it, but he saw no way to avoid the attempt to do it: He needed the Golden Fleece.

Jason said to King Aeetes, "I accept your challenge, as dangerous as it is. I was forced by one king to come here, and I am forced by another king to accept this challenge that may kill me."

King Aeetes replied, "Go back to your ship and companions and prepare yourself to accomplish the task or die trying. But if you decide not to attempt the task — if you refrain from trying to yoke the fire-breathing bulls or if you refrain from trying to kill the harvest of armed warriors — then I will do to you and your Argonauts things that will make other people refrain from coming here and asking for the Golden Fleece."

Jason knew that King Aeetes meant that all who had sailed here on the *Argo* would die.

Jason, Augeias, Telamon, and Argus left the king's halls. Argus had let his brothers know that for now they should stay behind. Chalciope feared the anger of her father, King Aeetes, and so she and her three sons who had stayed behind went to her chamber and avoided the king.

Jason was the most handsome of the four men as they left the king's hall, and Medea stared at him. Medea also left the king's hall and thought about Jason. She thought about his looks, his speech, his clothing, and his mannerisms. To her, Jason seemed to be the superior of every other man. But she was afraid for him because of the challenge that he had accepted. The fire-breathing bulls might kill him, the harvest of armed warriors might kill him, or King Aeetes might kill him.

A tear formed in the corner of her eye and rolled down her cheek, and she said to herself, "Why should I grieve over this man? Why should I grieve that he is going to die soon because he accepted the king's challenge? If he dies, I should not care, but I do care! Hecate, I am your priestess, and I pray to you to ask that you let him live and that you let him return safely to his home. But if the fire-breathing bulls must kill him, let him know that I grieve for him."

Argus had a plan that he shared with Jason and the others as they returned to the *Argo*, "This is a time of danger, and we must try to stay alive, using whatever means are necessary, even means that we might otherwise avoid. I have spoken before of Medea, a priestess of Hecate. Medea is a young sorceress who may be able to help you and protect you. I don't know whether my mother will want us to get Medea on our side, but I can talk to my mother. Unless we can get Medea on our side, we will all die here together. Therefore, I will go back and see my mother."

Jason replied, "In a little while, go and do that, but I feel bad because we must rely on a woman: Medea. I prefer to have my destiny in my own hands, not in the hands of a woman."

When Jason, Augeias, Telamon, and Argus reached the *Argo*, their companions greeted them and asked them questions. Jason said, "King Aeetes is definitely against us. For us to get the Golden Fleece, he has set a challenge for me. I must use two fire-breathing bulls to plow four acres. Then I must plant the teeth of a huge dragon. The teeth will produce a crop of armed warriors whom I must kill. All of this I must do in one day, or King Aeetes will not give us the Golden Fleece. I have accepted this challenge."

This challenge seemed impossible to accomplish to the Argonauts, and they stood silently. They despaired.

Peleus then said to the others, "We must decide what to do, although I doubt that talk will help us much. What will work best is action performed with strong arms. Jason, you have accepted the challenge and you should attempt to complete it if you are willing. However, do not make yourself do it if fear conquers you. If you are unwilling to make the attempt, I myself am willing to take your place. The worst that can happen to me is that I will die."

Other Argonauts volunteered to take Jason's place and try to complete the challenge: Telamon, Idas, Castor and Polydeuces, and Meleager, although he had just recently acquired the ability to grow a beard.

Argus said to the six brave men who had volunteered to take Jason's place, "Thank you for your bravery. I think, however, that we shall be able to get valuable help from my mother and from a young woman. My mother may be able to talk to Medea, who is both her own sister and a priestess of Hecate, and get her to help Jason. Medea knows spells and potions. She knows how to gather herbs and how to use them to put out a fire, stop a river from flooding, stop a star from falling, and hold the Moon in its place. I want to go back to the palace today and talk to my mother and see if she will talk to Medea and persuade her to help us."

The gods sent a favorable omen: A hawk pursued a dove, but the dove landed safely in Jason's lap, while the hawk, hurtling by in its great speed, impaled itself on a carving that decorated the *Argo*.

Mopsus, a seer, interpreted the omen: "This omen shows that Argus' plan will succeed. Jason's life will be in danger, but he will not die. The plans of King Aeetes will not succeed. This omen is backed up by the prophecy of Phineus, who told us that the goddess Aphrodite will be a most valuable ally for you. He also told us that whether our quest will be successful relies on her. The dove is the bird of Aphrodite, and so we ought to pray to Aphrodite and ask her for help."

The young Argonauts remembered what Phineus had told them, and so they supported this plan. However, Idas, who was overly outspoken, was completely against it. He shouted, "This is shameful! This plan relies on the help of a woman — Medea! Why should we rely on Aphrodite, goddess of love, rather than on Ares, god of war? We are men! Instead of relying on a woman to get us out of trouble, we should rely on our weapons and on our own strong arms and courage. But do as you wish. Be lovers, not warriors."

Many of the Argonauts were angry at Idas' words, but no one responded to him openly. Jason ignored Idas and said, "We are agreed to follow this plan. Argus will go to his mother and ask her to get Medea to help us."

However, Jason also did something that he knew Idas would approve of: He said, "We will bring the *Argo* out of its hiding place and anchor it where we can be seen. We ought not to hide any longer. After all, we are not afraid of fighting."

Argus left to see his mother, and the Argonauts moved the *Argo* to an anchorage point where the ship could be easily seen.

In the meantime, King Aeetes had summoned his men to a meeting. This was not held in the palace, but in a field. He was plotting against Jason and the Argonauts. He said, "Jason will die when he attempts to yoke the fire-breathing bulls to the plow. The bulls will kill him. After he is dead, we will cut the trees from a hillside and use the wood to burn the *Argo* and the Argonauts, who deserve to die because of their insolence. We have no need to make these people welcome here.

"True, I did provide hospitality to Phrixus when he came here on the golden ram, but I did that against my will, although Phrixus, a kind and gentle man, was in need of help. I helped Phrixus because I was following the orders of Zeus, who sent Hermes to me. If I would not of my own free will help a man like Phrixus, I certainly would not help Jason and the Argonauts, who are pirates and raiders. They want only to steal the property of my people, to ambush and kill them, and make raids and put other people's property on board their ship.

"In addition, we have to deal with the four sons of Phrixus. They brought Jason and the Argonauts here to overthrow me and take my crown. I once had a prophecy from my father, Helios, who warned me to beware of plots from members of my own family. Obviously, he was referring to my grandsons: the four sons of Phrixus. I will not kill them, but I will send them far away, to Greece. I do not need to fear any plots from my daughters, Chalciope and Medea, or from my son, Apsyrtus.

"Once Jason and the Argonauts are dead and the four sons of Phrixus have been banished from this land, all will be well. I order you to keep watch on Jason and the Argonauts and on the *Argo*. I do not want them to be able to escape their deaths."

Argus now reached King Aeetes' palace and talked to his mother, Chalciope, about persuading Medea to help them. Argus' three brothers were also present. Even before Argus suggested this plan to her, Chalciope had already thought of asking her sister, Medea the sorceress, for help. She had not yet asked her because of fear — her own and possibly Medea's. Medea might decline to help if she were afraid to make her father angry. Chalciope also feared that if Medea did agree to help them, King Aeetes might learn about the plot and punish everyone who participated in the plot.

As Argus and his mother talked, Medea lay in bed, asleep. Dreams came to her. She dreamed that Jason had accepted the challenge of King Aeetes not in order to win the Golden Fleece, but instead to win and marry her — Medea — and to take her back to his own land. Then she dreamed that it was not Jason who yoked the two fire-breathing bulls to the plow — she herself did that, easily. But after she had accomplished her father's challenge, her parents told her that it did not count — Jason, not Medea, had to accomplish the challenge. Jason and her father argued, and her father told her that she could make the decision as to who won. If she decided that her father had won, Medea would stay in Colchis, but if she decided that Jason had won, Medea would marry him and go with him to Iolcus. Medea dreamed that she immediately chose Jason as winner, angering her parents. As they screamed at her in her dream, she woke up.

She was afraid and looked around her. Slowly, she entered a fully awake state, and then she said to herself, "The coming of Jason and the Argonauts to Colchis will be a catastrophe. Jason should have stayed home and courted a local girl, never seeing me, who would then remain unmarried. But maybe I can help him. I will go to Chalciope, my older sister. She is worried about her four sons, and she may ask me to help them. By helping them, I can help Jason and keep him alive."

She got out of bed, and barefoot and in her nightgown she went to the door of her bedroom. She wanted to go to her sister and talk to her, but outside the door she hesitated, undecided about what she ought to do. She went back into her bedroom, and then she left her bedroom. She wanted to help Jason, but she feared making her father angry. Daughters ought to obey fathers, but she was a young woman in love.

After stepping out the door of her bedroom four times, yet failing to go to her sister, Medea fell face downward on her bed and cried. She was like a bride whose husband has died on their wedding day before they were able to enjoy each other on their wedding night. The bride will not join other women; instead, she sits alone in the bedroom that would have belonged to her husband and her, and she looks at the empty bed and grieves.

One of the female servants of the palace entered Medea's bedroom and saw her crying, and she ran to Chalciope to tell her what she had seen. Leaving her sons behind, Chalciope went immediately to Medea's bedroom to talk to her. Medea, still lying in bed, had scratched both of her cheeks, and tears ran down her cheeks.

Chalciope asked Medea, "Why are you crying? Are you ill? Have you heard bad news about my sons and me? Is our father going to harm them? I wish I lived far from here, somewhere where no one had ever heard of King Aeetes and the Colchians."

Medea did not answer immediately. She was embarrassed to admit that she loved Jason. She blushed. She tried to tell her sister the truth, but she could not make herself speak and admit that she loved Jason.

Finally, she said, "Chalciope, I am worried about what our father will do to your sons. I had a dream in which he did terrible things to them and to the strangers who have come here. May the gods stop such evil from ever occurring! May you never have to suffer such evil!"

Medea wanted her sister, Chalciope, to request help from her. Medea did not want to be the one to bring up Jason's name first.

As Medea had known would happen, Chalciope was horrified by Medea's "dream." Like all good mothers, Chalciope wanted her children to be safe. She said, "Like you, I have been afraid that bad things could happen to my sons. That is why I came here. I hoped that you and I might be able to come up with a plan to keep them safe. Swear to me that you will keep my words secret. Also swear to me that you will help me to keep my sons safe. Please do not do nothing and allow them to die. If you will not act to keep them safe, I swear that I will die with my sons and I will haunt you like a Fury that pursues someone who has committed an unavenged murder of a kinsperson."

Chalciope started to cry, and she knelt and put her arms around Medea's knees and pressed her face into Medea's lap. Medea also started to cry, and the few servants who were awake faintly heard the two mourning.

Medea said, "Chalciope, you need not speak of haunting me from the Land of the Dead. We will plan together what to do, and both of us hope that what we plan will save your sons. I swear by Heaven and Earth that I will help you by all means possible with whatever powers and knowledge I have."

Chalciope asked, "Can you do anything to help Jason? I am afraid that if Jason is killed, our father will then kill the Argonauts and either kill or banish my sons. If Jason stays alive, he will be an ally of my sons. Jason knows that he needs your help; he even sent my son Argus to me to ask me to ask you for your help. Argus is waiting for me to return and give him your decision."

Medea blushed. She was happy that Jason wanted her to help him. She said, "Chalciope, I will do whatever I can to help you and your sons. Your sons are like brothers to me; I was raised with them. You, my older sister, are like a mother to me. When I was an infant, you even breastfed me, as my mother has often told me. I will help Jason so that I can help you and your sons. In the morning, I will go to the temple of Hecate. I will have a potion that will keep Jason safe from the fire-breathing bulls. Tell your son Argus to tell Jason to meet me there."

Chalciope returned to her chamber and told her sons that Medea would help Jason and them.

Medea, however, suffered from emotional conflicts. She was planning to help Jason, a man whom her father opposed. Shouldn't she support her own father instead of supporting a stranger?

All was dark in the night. Sailors watched the stars. Travelers wanted to sleep, as did guards. Mothers mourning for their dead children found escape from pain and grief in sleep. Dogs did not bark. Men did not speak. All was quiet.

Medea stayed awake and thought about Jason. She imagined him trying to yoke the fire-breathing bulls. She imagined the bulls killing Jason. Her heart would not be still; it was like a reflection of sunlight from a pail in which water has just been poured — the reflection continually moves on a wall.

She pitied herself and cried. She agonized. She felt pain in her neck and throughout her body. Love often hurts.

At one moment, she thought that she would give Jason the potion that would protect him from the fire-breathing bulls. In the next moment, she thought that she would kill herself rather than go against her father's wishes. In the moment after that, she thought that she would do nothing and let events happen as they would without her taking action one way or the other.

Medea said to herself, "One choice will harm my father. If I harm my father, I also harm my mother. Another choice will harm Jason. Must I choose one of these evil choices?

"I would have been better off if the goddess Artemis had shot me with one of her arrows and sent me to the Land of the Dead before I had ever seen Jason. A Fury must have wanted to torment me and for that purpose brought Jason here. So let the fire-breathing bulls kill Jason if it is his fate to die! How should I prepare the potion that Jason needs to survive without my father and mother finding out what I have done? Would any plan I devise be able to keep my involvement secret? How could I face my parents after disobeying them?

Is there any possible way that I can help Jason without my parents learning what I have done? Should Jason and I meet — alone? Fate is against me. I am miserable now, with Jason alive. If Jason dies, I will be even more miserable. I am about to lose my reputation as a dutiful daughter. After I save Jason's life, he can go wherever he chooses, while I will kill myself by taking poison or by hanging myself. But that will not stop people from saying bad things about me, and not just the people here but also the people from all the cities in Colchis. They will talk about the girl who fell in love with a stranger and killed herself and disgraced her parents. I will have a bad reputation, and my parents will suffer. It would be better if I were to die here and now than to live and carry out my plan to help Jason."

Medea got out of bed and found the box in which she stored her herbs for making potions. Some herbs healed; some herbs killed. She cried as she thought about killing herself: She thought about swallowing a deadly poison and dying. She started to open the box, but then she thought about the sweetness of living and the bitterness of dying. The living can be happy and have happy friends. The living can see the Sun rise. Hera put these thoughts into Medea's head, and Medea set the box of herbs aside. She had made up her mind to help Jason.

Medea waited for dawn. She wanted to meet Jason and give him the potion that would save his life. She opened her door occasionally to see if the Sun was rising. When — finally — the glow of morning began to appear in the sky and people began to wake up, she felt happy.

Chalciope had told her sons what Medea had said she would do, and now Argus returned to the *Argo* to tell Jason the news. Argus told his brothers to stay behind with their mother in case other news arrived.

Medea, once the morning had fully arrived, put up her hair and washed her face. She anointed her skin with a soothing lotion, and she put a veil on her head. She was unaware of present evils and of evils yet to come.

Medea had twelve young, unwed, female servants, and she ordered them to yoke mules to the carriage that she drove to the Temple of Hecate. She then went to her box of herbs and potions and took out a potion that was named after Prometheus, who had stolen fire, given it to Humankind, and taught Humankind how to control it. This potion, combined with a sacrifice to Hecate, who has no siblings, will make a man who anoints his body with the potion invulnerable to fire and swords. It will also make a man courageous and strong. This potion is made from the flowers that spring up from the drops of ichor — the golden liquid that is the blood of the gods and other immortals — that fall to the ground when the eagle eats Prometheus' liver each day. To make the potion, Medea, in the darkness of night, had bathed seven times in seven streams and called three times on the name of Hecate, and then cut the flowers and took their sap. As she cut the flowers, the earth quaked and Prometheus moaned in pain.

Medea placed the potion in a belt she wore beneath her breasts, and then she went out to her carriage. She sat in the middle, with two female servants on each side, and she drove the carriage through the town and to the temple as the rest of her female servants followed beside the carriage.

As Medea and her female servants went through the town, passersby got out of the way of the carriage and were careful not to look Medea in the eye. Medea resembled Artemis after she has bathed in the Parthenius River and then stands in a chariot pulled by deer taking her to a sacrifice. Nymphs go with her and follow her chariot, but wild animals fear her.

Arriving at the Temple of Hecate, Medea told her female servants, "I have made a mistake, friends. We should not have come here — not while the strangers are anchored near our city. People in town are afraid of the strangers, and that is why no women have come to the temple today. But we are here, and we are alone, so let us enjoy ourselves. We can sing, we can dance, and we can pick flowers. Afterward, we can go back home.

"Listen to me. Today, you can get more than merely flowers. I have talked to my sister, Chalciope, and her son Argus, and they have told me that I will get gifts if I help Jason. Don't tell my father, please. Keep it a secret. I have agreed to help Jason face the fire-breathing bulls. I will meet Jason here today, and I will share the gifts with you, if he brings them. Then I will give him a potion — a potion more deadly than the one he expects to get from me. I do ask you, however, to let me speak to Jason alone."

Medea lied in some respects, but her lies worked.

Argus had told Jason that Medea had agreed to help him. Now he led Jason to the Temple of Hecate. With them was the seer Mopsus, who was able to give good advice to travellers and who was able to interpret the flight of birds and other omens sent by the gods. Mopsus felt that this day would end happily for Jason.

The gods have the power to enhance human beings, and Hera enhanced Jason. He was better looking that day than he had ever been or ever would be, and he was able to talk better on that day than on any other day of his life. Jason was like the starring male figure in a maiden's romantic daydream.

The gods also have the power to make animals speak and the power to make human beings understand what animals say. As the three men walked and arrived near the Temple of Hecate, Mopsus heard a crow in a poplar say, "This seer is not a seer if he does not know what even young girls know, that a maiden will not confess her love to a man if other people are present. This seer must leave Jason and Medea alone together. If he does not, he knows nothing of love and Aphrodite."

Mopsus heard the words of the crow, smiled, and said to Jason, "Go to the temple now and talk to Medea. The goddess Aphrodite will be your ally, as Phineus foretold. Argus and I will wait for you here. You and Medea must be alone."

This was good advice, and both Jason and Argus knew it.

Medea was singing and dancing with her female servants, but she was thinking about Jason. As she sang and danced, she kept looking to see if Jason had arrived. Sometimes, she heard the wind and thought that Jason had arrived.

Soon, Jason did arrive. He looked like Sirius, the brightest star at night. Sirius is beautiful, but its arrival in the night sky over Greece comes when the long, hot, dry summer comes. Plants wilt, men grow weaker, and women often become overly aroused. Sirius is beautiful, but it is dangerous. Like Sirius, Jason was beautiful — and dangerous for Medea. She blushed, and she could not move toward or away from him. Her female servants remembered that Medea had said that she wanted to be alone with Jason, and so they left them and waited at a distance.

Silent, Medea and Jason stood close to each other. They were like pines on a day when the wind does not blow. But when the wind blows, then the pines are not silent but seem to speak.

Jason looked at Medea for a while, noticing her discomfort, and then he said to her, "I am alone. You need not be afraid of me. I am not an evil man, as I know that some men are. I was not evil back home, in my own country. Please ask — or tell — me anything you wish. You and I are friends, and we are at a temple, where you are under the protection of Hecate, the goddess you serve.

I am not the type of man who would disrespect a goddess or holy ground or priestess.

"You have told your sister that you would help me by giving me a magic potion that will keep me safe. I beg you by the goddess you serve and by your parents to give me that potion. I beg you in the name of Zeus, the god who protects suppliants. I am a suppliant — I am a stranger who is in danger here. Zeus also protects guests, and I have eaten in your father's palace. I ask you to help me. Unless you and your sister help me, I will never be able to accomplish the task that King Aeetes, your father, has set for me. I will never be able to yoke the fire-breathing bulls to the plow, and I will never be able to kill the fully armored warriors who grow from the seeds that are the dragon's teeth. Help me, and I will praise you in distant lands. So will the Argonauts. So will their wives and mothers and sisters and daughters — women who wait for us, fearful that we have died and will never return home.

"Remember Ariadne. She is the daughter of Minos and Pasiphae. She is your cousin because Pasiphae is the sister of King Aeetes, your father. Ariadne helped Theseus when he needed help. Minos is the King of Crete, and he demanded tribute from Athens because his son had been murdered in Athens. Minos demanded that the Athenians send him every nine years seven young men and seven young women as tribute. These young people Minos sent into a labyrinth, where the Minotaur — a half-bull, half-human monster — devoured them. Theseus volunteered to be one of the young men sent as tribute to the island of Crete. His plan was to kill the Minotaur and stop the requirement of sending Athenian young people to Crete as tribute. Ariadne helped Theseus by giving him a ball of string to use to find his way out of the labyrinth. Theseus tied one end of the string to the entrance to the labyrinth, then entered the labyrinth and killed the Minotaur. He then followed the string back to the entrance of the labyrinth. Theseus made peace with King Minos and sailed away with Ariadne, who is loved by the gods. She even has stars in the night sky that are called Ariadne's Crown. Be like Ariadne. Save my friends and me the way that Ariadne saved Theseus. I will thank you. You are beautiful, and I think that your beauty reveals that you have a kind heart."

All that Jason told Medea about Ariadne was true, but he left out one important fact. After Theseus and Ariadne ran away together, Theseus abandoned her on an island. A young woman can put her faith in a hero, and yet the hero may not treat her well.

Medea listened to the words that Jason spoke, and she did not think about the one important fact that Jason had not spoken. She smiled as she looked at him. She was not sure what to say to him, but she gave him the magic potion she carried in her belt. He gladly took it from her — it would keep him alive. She was happy that he needed her help and happy that she could help him. She wanted to tell him many things. Jason's face seemed to her to be alight with love. Medea's heart melted like frost on a rose melts in the morning Sun. She wanted to give Jason her soul.

Embarrassed, Jason and Medea looked at the ground. Then they looked at each other again.

Medea said, "Let me tell you how to keep yourself alive. My father will meet with you and will give you the teeth of the dragon to plant in the field you plow by using the fire-breathing bulls. After you get the teeth of the dragon, wait until midnight and then bathe alone in a river that always flows and never dries up due to drought. After you bathe, dress in dark clothing and dig a round pit and fill it with wood. Then kill a ewe and burn all of it as a sacrifice to Hecate. Also give Hecate honey and prayers. Afterward, leave and do not look behind you even if you hear footsteps behind you or the barking of dogs. If you look behind you, you and your friends will almost certainly die.

"When morning arrives, strip and rub this magic potion onto your body as if the potion were oil. When you do, you will feel yourself grow stronger and more courageous. You will feel that you can conquer not only men, but also the gods themselves. Sprinkle the magic potion onto your sword, shield, and spear. Once you have done this, you will not be harmed by the fire of the bulls or by the weapons of the men who will be born from the earth. The magic potion, however, will last for only one day. During that time, do not be afraid.

"After you have yoked the fire-breathing bulls and plowed the field and planted the teeth of the dragon, watch as the fully armed men grow from the earth. Wait until some of the men are fully grown and out of the soil and then throw a heavy stone among them. They will begin to fight over the stone the way that hungry dogs fight over food. They will begin to kill each other. At that moment, join them and kill them.

"After all of the fully armed men are dead due to you or to each other, you can get the Golden Fleece and take it back to your home, which is, I think, far from Aea, my city. Go there or wherever you want to go when you sail away."

Medea then looked at the ground and wept as she imagined Jason sailing away from her. She then looked at him and held his hand. She was in love.

Medea said, "Remember me after you leave. Remember my name. I will remember you and your name. Now tell me about your home, and tell me about where you will sail when you leave here. Will you sail by Orchomenus, a wealthy city? Will you sail by the island of Aea? And tell me more about famous Ariadne, the daughter of Pasiphae, my father's sister."

Jason felt love for Medea as he told her, "If I live to reach again my homeland, assuming that King Aeetes does not give me an even harder task that will kill me, I know one thing: I will never forget you. Both at day and at night, I will remember you in my homeland.

"My homeland has mountains bordering it. It has sheep and pastureland. My homeland gave birth to Deucalion, one of the mortal sons of Prometheus. Deucalion was civilized. He was the first man to do such things as found cities and build temples and rule over men as their king. My homeland is named Thessaly. In this land is the city from which I came: Iolcus. Many other cities are there. From my homeland came the man who founded the wealthy city of Orchomenus.

"About Ariadne, I can say that her father, King Minos, eventually became reconciled to her and to Theseus. I hope that your father, King Aeetes, will eventually become reconciled to you and to me."

Jason had hoped to sooth Medea with these words, but instead she felt pessimistic and said to him, "In your homeland and throughout Greece, people may behave ethically, but my father is much different. He is not like the forgiving King Minos you describe, and I cannot claim to be as good a person as Ariadne. I cannot see my father becoming reconciled with you.

"But, at least, you can remember me when you are home and I can remember you even if my parents do not become reconciled with you. However, perhaps a day will come when a bird shall bring me a message — a message that you have forgotten me. If that happens, I hope that a storm wind will sweep me into the air and carry me — unexpected — to you so that I can denounce you face to face for forgetting me — the person who saved your life."

As Medea spoke, she wept.

Jason said to her, "I will never forget you. You will never receive a visit from a message-bearing bird, and the storm winds will never lift you into the air and carry you to me. If you come to my homeland, you will be respected and honored by all — women as well as men. They will treat you as a goddess because you will have saved not only my life, but also the lives of their husbands and sons and brothers and fathers. And you and I shall be married and share a bed. We will love each other and share our lives together until Death carries us to the Land of the Dead."

Medea thought happily of marriage to Jason, but she disliked having been disloyal to her father by giving Jason the potion. But Medea did not mention marriage. She did not know what the future would bring. Hera, like all gods and goddesses, knew the futures of mortals. Hera knew that Medea and Jason would soon be married. Medea would leave her homeland and live in Jason's homeland, and she would be the one who would punish King Pelias, who had disrespected Hera.

From a distance, Medea's young female servants had been watching her and Jason. Now the servants were restless because it was growing late and very soon Medea needed to go to her home and her mother. Medea did not think about leaving. She thought only of Jason and how handsome he was and the words he spoke to her.

Jason, however, realized that it was growing late, and he said to Medea, "We must go now, before the Sun sets. We ought to avoid the curiosity of passersby who may see us if we stay here. But let us meet again here soon."

Medea and Jason knew each other now. They parted. Jason, happy, walked back to Argus and Mopsus and then they walked to the *Argo*. Medea's young female servants joined her. Medea, however, kept thinking about Jason; she ignored her servants. Automatically, without thinking about what she was doing, she climbed onto the carriage, took the whip in her hand, and started back to her father's palace with her servants.

In the palace, her sister, Chalciope, asked her questions. Chalciope wanted to be sure that her sons would be safe. But Medea was not in a mood to talk. She ignored her sister, and sat. She rested her cheek on her hand, and she cried as she thought about having been disloyal to her father.

As Jason, Argus, and Mopsus walked to the *Argo*, he told them all that had happened. When they arrived at the *Argo*, Jason repeated his story to the other Argonauts, and they rejoiced because Medea had given Jason the magic potion. Idas continued to sulk, away from the others, but the other Argonauts rejoiced.

The next morning, Telamon and Aethalides, a son of Hermes to whom Hermes had given an infallible memory, served as heralds and went to King Aeetes to get the dragon teeth that Jason would sow. These teeth, which King Aeetes gave the heralds, were those of a dragon that Cadmus had slain in Thebes. Zeus had kidnapped Europa, Cadmus' sister, and he ran away with her. Cadmus set off on a quest to find Europa, but the Oracle of Delphi commanded him to abandon that search and instead to found a city. The Oracle commanded Cadmus to follow a cow until it lay down. Wherever it lay down was the spot that Cadmus should found his city. That city was Thebes, and to get citizens for his city, Cadmus had to slay a dragon and sow its teeth, which grew into warriors. After Cadmus had slain the dragon, the goddess Athena extracted its teeth and gave half to Cadmus and half to King Aeetes.

King Aeetes gave the dragon's teeth to Telamon and Aethalides. King Aeetes was convinced that Jason would die when he attempted to perform the challenge that King Aeetes had given him. Even if Jason succeeded in plowing the field with the fire-breathing bulls, the warriors who would grow from the teeth of the dragon would kill him.

Evening arrived, and Jason waited for night. In night's darkness and quiet, he went out alone from the *Argo* and walked across a plain, carrying everything he needed to perform the rite that Medea had told him to perform. Most of the items had come from the *Argo*, but Argus, the son of King Aeetes, had brought him milk and a ewe. In an always-flowing river, Jason bathed, alone, and then he put on a cloak that was a gift from Hypsipyle, his lover on the island of Lemnos, who wanted Jason to remember her and the love they had made together.

Jason then dug a trench and sacrificed the ewe and honey to Hecate, and he prayed to her and asked for her help during the following day. He moved away from the sacrifice, and Hecate in person came out of the Land of the Dead to accept it. The wreath she wore on her head was composed of live snakes and oak branches, a thousand torches burned around her, and dogs from the Land of the Dead surrounded her and barked. Jason was afraid, and the nymphs of the river screamed in fear. Despite his fear, when Jason left, he did not look behind him.

Jason reached the *Argo*, and he waited for dawn.

At dawn, King Aeetes prepared himself to witness how Jason would respond to the challenge that King Aeetes had set for him. King Aeetes put on a cuirass — a piece of armor consisting of a breastplate and a backplate fastened together. Ares killed the giant Mimas in the battle between gods and giants, and then he gave King Aeetes this cuirass. King Aeetes also put on his golden, four-plated helmet that gleamed like the Sun as it rises over the Ocean. He also lifted his shield and his spear. None of the Argonauts, now that they lacked Heracles, could be victorious against that spear. Only Heracles could have conquered the man who wielded that spear.

King Aeetes' son, Phaeton, stood outside, holding the reins of the horses that were harnessed to his father's chariot. King Aeetes climbed into the chariot, took the reins, and then drove to the field that Jason was supposed to plow. Crowds of people were moving to that field. King Aeetes resembled Poseidon and his chariot as he drove to the field.

Jason followed Medea's instructions. He anointed his shield, spear, and sword with the magic potion. The Argonauts knew that the magic potion was supposed to make the shield and weapons invincible, and so they tested them. They tried to break Jason's spear, but they could not even bend it. Idas, still angry, was unconvinced. He took out his sword and attacked Jason's spear, but his sword bounced off the shaft of Jason's spear the way that a blacksmith's hammer bounces off his anvil. The Argonauts rejoiced; they were convinced that Jason would meet King Aeetes' challenge.

Jason now anointed his own body with the magic potion. He felt himself growing much stronger, and he did not fear the upcoming challenge. His fingers twitched in anticipation the way that a warhorse anticipates a battle and prances in excitement. To prepare himself for the tasks that lay ahead of him, Jason leapt and fought a mock battle. His shield and the point of his spear flashed the way that lightning flashes in a storm.

Now it was time to go to the field that Jason would plow. The Argonauts rowed the *Argo* to the field of Ares past the city of Aea. It was as far from the city as is the turning post of a chariot race held to honor a king in his funeral games. King Aeetes and many Colchians were waiting for them; King Aeetes was still in his chariot.

Jason jumped on the shore and went to the plain. He had his shield, spear, and sword. He carried a shiny helmet that was made of bronze and held the sharp teeth of the dragon; his sword hung in a scabbard that was slung over his shoulder. He did not wear armor. His body was bare, like the body of the god Apollo, but he carried weapons, like Ares, the god of war.

Jason looked around the field of Ares and saw the steel plow and the bronze yoke. He stuck his spear in the ground and left behind his helmet and the teeth of the dragon as he searched the ground for signs of the fire-breathing bulls. He carried his shield in his hands.

The bulls came up out of their lair in the ground, and when they snorted, fire came from their mouths and nostrils. Jason held up his shield as the bulls charged him. The Argonauts were terrified, but Jason held his ground as the bulls butted his shield. He did not move even an inch backward. Fire spewed from the bulls like fire spews when a blacksmith blows it with his bellows. The heat attacked him like lightning attacks an unlucky man, but Medea's magic potion was more powerful than the fire.

Jason grabbed one of the bulls by the end of a horn and forced it to go to the plow. He kicked the bronze legs of the bull and forced it to its knees. The other bull charged at Jason, but he also forced it to its knees. Jason tossed aside his shield, and he held both bulls down as their fire surrounded his body. Jason's strength amazed King Aeetes.

Castor and Polydeuces picked up the bronze yoke and gave it to Jason, who fastened it and the plow to the bulls. Castor and Polydeuces then backed away from the fire-breathing bulls and rejoined the other Argonauts while Jason picked up his spear and grabbed his helmet. He used his spear to prick the bulls and guide them as they pulled the plow.

Furious, the bulls bellowed and spurted fire, but they obeyed Jason and his spear. Jason stood on the plow to make it dig deep in the earth, and he sowed the furrows with the dragon's teeth, frequently looking back in case the fully armored men should sprout quickly and attack him. The bulls plowed for two-thirds of the day, and then the plowing and sowing were done. All four acres of the field had been sowed with dragon's teeth. It was now the time when weary farmers hope to release their oxen from the yoke.

Jason released the fire-breathing bulls from the yoke, and they ran away. He surveyed the field, but he saw no sprouting warriors, and so he went to the Argonauts, who praised what he had accomplished. Thirsty from the fire of the bulls and from the labor of plowing, Jason dipped his helmet into the river and drank. Knowing that soon he would fight, he warmed his muscles by flexing them. He also mentally prepared himself for the coming combat. He worked himself into a frenzy. He was like a boar that prepares to kill men by sharpening its tusks and becoming so angry that foam drips from its mouth.

Now the armed warriors began to sprout. Coming up from the ground were men, helmets, shields, spears, and swords. The armor and weapons gleamed in the Sun; the gods on Mount Olympus saw flashes of light coming from the field of Ares. The glints looked like stars shining in the sky in the winter when winds have blown away the clouds that have deposited snow on the fields.

Jason remembered the commands of Medea. He picked up a huge boulder that Ares was capable of throwing by himself but that four strong men of today could not lift. Jason threw the huge boulder among the warriors springing from the ground — King Aeetes was amazed at how far Jason threw the boulder. The fully armed warriors rushed to the boulder and attacked each other as other warriors continued to grow in the ground. The warriors fought each other like dogs. They yelled and attacked and killed each other. They fell like trees fall when attacked by a hurricane.

Jason then joined the battle and killed warriors. Like a meteor, he rushed to the battle, carrying his sword. He killed and killed again. He killed warriors who were still growing in the ground, and he killed warriors who had fully emerged from the ground. A farmer may decide to harvest unripe corn because of a war in which the enemy may steal unharvested ripe corn from him. Like that farmer, Jason killed unripe, not fully grown warriors. Like water fills a channel, the blood of the warriors whom Jason slew filled the furrows of the field. Many warriors died with part of their bodies still in the ground. Warriors fell on their faces, or their backs, or their sides. They died like saplings in an orchard die when a terrific storm snaps them in two, ruining the work of the gardener and impoverishing the owner of the orchard.

King Aeetes watched all, and he was not happy. He and his people went back to the city of Aea, and he plotted against Jason and the Argonauts. Jason had met the challenge, but King Aeetes still wanted him to die.

The Sun set. Jason's day of invulnerability was over, but he had accomplished what needed to be done: He had met King Aeetes' challenge.

Chapter 4: Acquisition of the Golden Fleece and the Journey Home

King Aeetes did not sleep; he stayed awake and plotted against Jason and the Argonauts. He was angry, and he suspected that his daughters had helped Jason.

Medea was afraid — Hera made her feel fear. She was like a fawn, hidden in the woods, that hears the baying of hounds as they hunt. She trembled. She knew that her father must suspect or know what she had done to help Jason. She knew that her father would punish her. Her blood rushed through her veins, and she could hear her rushing blood. Her eyes hurt. She groaned, she tightly grasped her throat, and she pulled her hair.

Medea thought about committing suicide by swallowing poison, and she got her box of herbs, both healing and hurting, and took out some of the poisonous herbs, but Hera made her think instead about running away. The four sons of Phrixus were also in danger; they could flee with her. The thought of escape calmed her; she grew strong.

Medea put the poisonous herbs back in the box. She was ready to say farewell to her old life and begin a new life. She kissed her bed and the doorposts of her room. She gently stroked the walls of her room. She cut off a lock of her hair and left it behind for her mother as a memento. She said, "Mother, I am going far away. Farewell. Chalciope, farewell. Home, farewell. Major changes have come into my life. Perhaps it would have been better if Jason had never come here. Perhaps it would have been better if Jason had drowned in the sea."

Medea wept, much like a girl weeps who was born into a rich family but who suffered a change in fortune because of war or pirates and had recently become a slave-girl.

Medea then ran through the palace, chanting magic orders that opened doors for her before she reached them. She was barefoot, and she ran down narrow streets with one hand holding up her cloak to hide her face and her other hand holding up the bottom of her skirt so she would not trip on it. She ran through the city, taking less-populated routes, and she ran outside the city, past the walls, without the guard recognizing or even seeing her. She was running to the *Argo*. She knew the way well; she was accustomed to search in this area for corpses and herbs to use in her work as a sorceress. She was afraid as she ran.

The goddess Moon, daughter of the Titans Hyperion and Theia, saw Medea, realized that she was in love, and laughed. She said to herself, "Like me, you are in love. I fell in love with the mortal shepherd Endymion, and I asked that he be given eternal youth so that I could admire his beauty forever. By doing that, I did not act the way that an immortal goddess ought to act — immortal goddesses ought not to fall in love with mortal men. And now you are in love with a man whom you ought not to love — you ought to be obeying your father and doing his wishes, not the wishes of Jason. Often, Medea, you have had power over me. In order to do magic, you have often made the night cloudy so that my light would not reveal your actions. And now love has power over you. Eros, the son of Aphrodite, has made you fall in love in Jason, and he will bring you many heartaches. Run, Medea. Run fast, but you will not outrun sighs and unhappiness, although you are a sorceress."

Medea kept running and reached the river where the *Argo* was anchored. She looked across the river and saw the bonfire that the Argonauts had built on the shore to celebrate Jason's triumph in King Aeetes' challenge. The four sons of Chalciope were with Jason and the Argonauts. She shouted to Phrontis, her cousin, the youngest son of Phrixus. He and others recognized her voice, and he shouted back to her. She shouted three times so that they could find her in the darkness, and the Argonauts rowed the *Argo* over to her.

Jason jumped from the deck of the *Argo* onto the riverbank. Phrontis and Argus, Medea's cousins, followed him. Medea put her arms in supplication around the knees of her cousins, and she pleaded, "Save both me and yourselves from the punishment of King Aeetes! He knows everything! He knows how Jason was able to meet his challenge! Let us sail away from him before he can punish us! Let us go to the Golden Fleece and take it. I can put the guardian snake to sleep.

"Jason, you must vow to help me and to protect me. Vow to the gods that you will not let me be mistreated and you will not let me be without a protector when we leave my country and go to your country."

She fell before Jason in supplication.

Jason raised her from the ground, hugged her, and said, "I swear to Zeus and Hera that when we reach my own country I will marry you and make you my wife."

Medea then urged Jason and the Argonauts to sail to the tree on which hung the Golden Fleece. Night was the best time to seize the Golden Fleece and flee from King Aeetes. Everyone, including Medea, boarded the *Argo*, and the Argonauts rowed to the sacred grove of Ares.

Medea panicked. She thought of returning home. She held out her hands to the riverbank they were leaving behind, but Jason noticed her distress and comforted her.

They arrived at their destination before dawn, at the time when a hunter rises to go hunting with a hound before the Sun rises and his quarry goes into hiding. Argus, son of Phrixus, advised that Medea and Jason depart from the *Argo* at the location known as the Ram's Bed, which is where the Golden Ram landed with Phrixus and where Phrixus had sacrificed the Golden Ram as Hermes had instructed him to do. Medea and Jason followed Argus' advice.

They followed a path to the sacred wood where the Golden Fleece hung from a tree. The Golden Fleece was bright like a cloud that has been colored by the Sun at dawn. The huge snake that guarded the Golden Fleece with its never-sleeping eyes saw them and hissed at them. The hiss traveled a far distance, and it startled babies. Mothers held their babies closer and hugged them.

The snake came closer to Medea and Jason, but Medea began to chant, invoking the god of Sleep to come and overpower the snake. She also invoked the dreaded goddess Hecate. Jason, terrified, stood behind Medea. The snake, hearing Medea's words, began to relax its body, but its head swayed over Medea and Jason and threatened to swallow them.

Medea, still chanting, dipped some freshly cut juniper in a potion and sprinkled the snake's eyes with her magic. The eyes that had never slept before now slept. The snake's head and body lay on the ground, overcome by the scent of the magic potion. Following Medea's orders, Jason got the Golden Fleece from the tree while Medea continued to anoint the snake's head with her magic potion. Jason called to her that he had gotten the Golden Fleece, and she left the snake as it slept.

Jason lifted the Golden Fleece and looked at it. It shimmered. It cast a light that illuminated his face. He was as happy as a girl whose gown beautifully reflects the light of the Moon as it climbs the night sky and shines into her bedroom. The Golden Fleece was as large as the hide of a yearling heifer. It was heavy, and the light that came from it illuminated the path on which he and Medea walked. Sometimes, he slung it over his shoulder and it reached to his feet. Sometimes, he made it into a bundle that he carried in his arms. Finally, Jason had the Golden Fleece, but now he was afraid that a god or a robber might take it from him.

At dawn, Jason and Medea rejoined the Argonauts, who marveled at the Golden Fleece, which shone like the lightning of Zeus. The Argonauts wanted to touch it, but Jason stopped them and covered the Golden Fleece with a new cloak.

Jason found a seat for Medea and then told the Argonauts, "Friends, let us leave right away. With the help of Medea, whom I intend to take home and marry if she consents, we have the Golden Fleece for which we have endured so much. Medea has given us much help for which all of us ought to be thankful.

"We must leave quickly because King Aeetes and his men must be on their way to capture and punish us. Let two men row on each bench, and let half of us arm ourselves and hold our shields in readiness to protect all of us in case of arrows. We can take turns rowing.

"What we do now will have an effect on our homeland. Will King Pelias be punished for wrongfully taking the crown from my father? Medea has helped us get what we need to punish King Pelias and take his crown. What we do now will either free Thessaly or make its citizens grieve."

Jason put on his armor as the Argonauts applauded him, and all set sail. Jason stood beside Medea and Ancaeus, the *Argo*'s pilot. The other Argonauts rowed quickly down the river so they could reach the sea and flee.

King Aeetes and his men had learned all that Medea had done to help Jason. They also knew that Medea loved Jason. Having armed themselves, they met in the marketplace. The armed men were as numerous as waves whipped up by wind or as leaves that fall to the ground in autumn.

King Aeetes was in his chariot. In one hand he held a round shield, and in his other hand he held a pinewood torch. Pointing forward, his spear lay in his chariot. Apsyrtus, his son, served as his charioteer. Apsyrtus held the reins of the horses that Helios had given to King Aeetes.

The *Argo*, however, had reached the sea, making its capture much more difficult and angering King Aeetes. Furious, he prayed to Helios and to Zeus and told them how he believed that he had been mistreated. Furious, he told his men that they must find Medea — or suffer terrible consequences for failing. Wherever they found Medea — on land or at sea — they must take her to him so that she could pay for her crimes against him and so that he could get revenge on her. The penalty for failing to bring back Medea? Death.

As King Aeetes threatened them, his men loaded and then launched the ships. They were as numerous as the birds that fly in swarms over the sea.

Hera sent the Argonauts a favorable wind; she wanted Medea to reach Thessaly so that King Pelias could be punished for offering sacrifices to all the gods and goddesses except Hera. On the third morning, Jason and the Argonauts stopped at the mouth of a river so that Medea could perform a sacrifice to Hecate. The details of that sacrifice must not be revealed.

The river was located in the land of the Paphlagonians, which was next to the land of the Mariandyni. Dascylus, the son of King Lycus of the Mariandyni, was close to home.

Now Jason and the Argonauts thought about what route they should take. The seer Phineus had told them that they would return to Thessaly by a route different from the one they had taken to depart from Thessaly, but what that different route would be they did not know.

Argus, the oldest son of Phrixus, said, "My brothers and I were originally traveling to Orchomenus in Boeotia, Greece. We know of an alternate route to Orchomenus and to Thessaly that priests from Thebes, Egypt, mapped. Early in the history of humanity, a king from Egypt traveled throughout Europe and Asia with a great army and he founded many cities, some of which still exist, although many have disappeared. Among the cities that survived is Aea, the city of King Aeetes. The people there are descended from the Egyptians. In the city of Aea are stone tablets that the original settlers engraved with maps. These maps show the Ister River, which is big enough and deep enough for ships to sail in. The Ister, which is connected to the Ocean that surrounds all land, has its source in the far north, flows south, and divides into two branches at the border of Thrace and Scythia. One branch flows into the Black Sea, and the other branch flows into the sea east of Italy. We can sail up the branch that empties into the Black Sea and make our way up the river and then sail down the branch that empties into the sea east of Italy."

This was the route that Phineus had foreknown that Jason and the Argonauts would use to return home. The goddess Hera gave them a sign: a long-lasting trail of light across the sky. Jason and the Argonauts rejoiced at the sign: They now knew the route that they should take to return home.

Dascylus, the son of King Lycus, had sailed with Jason and the Argonauts to the city of Aea. Now Jason and the Argonauts left him behind — close to his father — and they sailed away to the Ister River.

Some of King Aeetes' men had sailed between the Clashing Rocks and out of the Black Sea. They were mistaken about where the *Argo* was sailing.

The remaining ships, under the command of Apsyrtus, King Aeetes' son, sailed for the Ister River. This river divided into two channels that emptied into the Black Sea: the Fair Mouth and the Narex. Apsyrtus and his ships sailed up the Fair Mouth, which was the shorter way. The *Argo* sailed up the Narex. Apsyrtus and his ships reached the main channel of the Ister River before the *Argo* did.

The ships under the command of Apsyrtus panicked all who saw them, for none of the people here had ever seen a ship. Shepherds fled, leaving their sheep behind. The shepherds thought that the ships were sea monsters.

When Apsyrtus and his ships reached the main channel of the Ister River, they sailed far up the river to the place where the river flowed down from the Ocean and divided into two channels that flowed to two seas: the Black Sea and the sea east of Italy. They took the channel that flowed to the sea east of Italy and there they took positions to prevent the *Argo* from escaping. Two islands in the river were sacred to Artemis, daughter of Zeus, and none of Apsyrtus' ships landed on them out of respect to the goddess. One of the islands had a temple that was dedicated to Artemis; the other island did not. Jason and the Argonauts landed on the island that did not have a temple. The men of Apsyrtus occupied all of the islands except the two that were dedicated to Artemis.

If Jason and the Argonauts had been forced to fight Apsyrtus and his men, who greatly outnumbered them, Jason and the Argonauts would have died, so they instead used diplomacy. The leaders of the groups met and decided that

Jason and the Argonauts ought to have the Golden Fleece because King Aeetes had set a challenge for Jason and told him that he could have the Golden Fleece if he met the challenge. That Jason had taken the Golden Fleece secretly, by night, did not matter because it belonged to him.

The two groups disagreed over Medea. They decided that Jason and the Argonauts would take Medea to the temple of Artemis and leave her there until a local leader would decide which group should get custody of Medea. That leader would decide whether she would go back to King Aeetes, her father, or whether she should go with Jason and the Argonauts.

When Medea learned what the leaders of the two groups had decided, she was unhappy. She talked to Jason privately: "Why are you and Apsyrtus — my brother — debating about me? Haven't you promised me that you will marry me? Have you forgotten the promises you made to me when you needed my help to stay alive and to get the Golden Fleece? Have you forgotten the oaths you made to Zeus? Have you forgotten the promises you made that I believed in when I acted like a disobedient daughter and disobeyed my father? Have you forgotten the promises you made that I believed in when I left my home, my family, and my homeland? Now I am far from home with only winged halcyons for company. I am suffering because I helped you stay alive and get the Golden Fleece. To help you, I disobeyed my father's wishes.

"You ought to treat me as your daughter, your wife, your sister. I am going with you to your home. You need to protect me and stay with me, not participate in councils in which men argue that I ought to be taken back to my father, who will severely punish me. Why shouldn't you and I run away together — now? We are engaged to be lawfully married. Either keep your promises to me or cut my throat with your sword. Give me whichever reward you think I deserve.

"What will happen to me if my brother takes me back to my father? How will my father treat me? As a dutiful daughter? No. Think of the punishments I will be forced to endure. Think of the cruel tortures.

"And what about you? You must be anticipating a happy return home. I hope that Hera will not permit you to return to your home. I hope that you will endure misery and that you think of me. I hope that you lose the Golden Fleece and that it disappears the way a dream disappears. I hope that the Golden Fleece finds its way down into the Land of the Dead. I hope that the Furies punish you for what you have done to me and that the Furies give me satisfaction. You have made — and you are ready to break — solemn oaths, and the Furies will be on my side, not on yours.

"I will soon teach you not to break your oaths."

Medea was close to setting the *Argo* on fire and killing herself in the flames.

Jason was afraid of Medea and of how the raging sorceress might punish him. He attempted to calm her.

Jason said to her, "I also do not want to be a diplomat and bargain with your brother, but I have no choice. Your brother's men greatly outnumber my men, and I am trying to avoid a battle that will leave all of the Argonauts and me dead. Not only do the forces of your brother outnumber me, but also the people in these lands support him and are ready to fight alongside him. Would it help you if all of us were killed?

"The truce that we have made has bought us time in which to plan a trick that will free all of us, including you. If we can somehow get rid of your brother, I think that the forces opposing us will lose their motivation to fight and kill us. But if the Argonauts and I have to fight those forces, we will."

Medea's reply was bloodthirsty: "So let us now plan a trick. One evil deed leads to another. I was disloyal to my father when I helped you. That is one evil deed. Now let me do another evil deed. Keep the peace for now, and I will trick my brother and deliver him to you. You can help in the deception by giving him gifts. As his men take the gifts away, I will secretly give his heralds a message telling him to return later to the temple of Artemis so that he and I can plot together to get the Golden Fleece away from you so that then my brother and me can return to our home. If you want to, you can kill my brother — we are in a desperate situation — and if you want to, you can fight the men he brings with him to the island on which the temple of Artemis is located."

Jason and Medea decided to set the trap for her brother. Jason gave him many gifts, including a purple robe that Hypsipyle, Jason's lover on Lemnos, had given to him. The Graces had made the purple robe for the god Dionysus, who had given it to Thoas, his son. Thoas had given it to Hypsipyle, his daughter, who gave it and other gifts to Jason when he left the island of Lemnos. This purple robe pleased the senses of sight and of touch. Even its scent was pleasant. On this purple robe, the god Dionysus, inebriated by drinking wine and nectar, had lain as he had sex with Ariadne on the island of Dia after Theseus had abandoned her there. Ariadne gave birth to Thoas.

Medea set up a meeting with her brother by giving his heralds a message: He was to go to the temple of Artemis at night. Medea would already be there, and they could plot how they could get the Golden Fleece — Medea stated that she was planning to steal it — and return to their home. Medea also told the heralds that Jason and the Argonauts had forced her to leave her home. In addition to using words to trick her brother, she used magic spells and drugs that she tossed to the four winds. These spells and drugs were so powerful that Medea could have — if she had wanted — persuaded wild animals from far away to leave their lairs and come to the temple of Artemis.

Love for Jason made Medea commit an act of enormous evil. Eros had caused such love.

Medea was in the temple of Artemis that night. Jason hid in the temple and waited for Apsyrtus, Medea's brother, to arrive. The Argonauts would land on the island later that night.

Apsyrtus, hoping to trick Jason and get both the Golden Fleece and Medea, landed on the island with some men, whom he left behind as he walked to the temple and conferred with his sister. In plotting with the treacherous Medea, he was a like a small boy trying to do what brave men could not. He was like a small boy trying to cross a dangerous river when brave men would not dare to make the attempt.

Medea pretended to plot against Jason, and Apsyrtus thought that they had come up with a good plan, but Jason came out from his hiding place and raised his sword high. Medea turned away and covered her eyes with her veil — she did not want to witness the death of her brother.

Jason struck down Apsyrtus the way that a butcher strikes down a bull. Apsyrtus sank to his knees. He knew that he would die, and he put his hands down to his wound to make them bloody, and then he wiped his blood on Medea's veil and robe.

This slaughter took place in the temple — a great outrage. This slaughter of a brother was instituted by his sister — a great outrage. This slaughter was treacherous — a great outrage. One of the Furies who punish treacherous murders — especially the murders of one kinsman or kinswoman by another — witnessed the murder.

Jason, wanting to avoid the pollution of his murder, performed a rite: He cut off the hands, feet, nose, and ears of Apsyrtus. One purpose of this rite was to prevent the spirit of the murdered man from pursuing vengeance for his murder. Another purpose was to offer the corpse to the gods in the Land of the Dead. Jason also performed a second rite in an attempt to expiate the pollution of his act. Three times, he licked up some of Apsyrtus' blood and spat it out. Murderers often perform these rites. Then Jason buried the corpse.

Medea used a torch to signal the Argonauts, and they landed the *Argo* near the ship that had brought her brother to the island. The Argonauts slaughtered the crew of her brother's ship. They were like hawks attacking pigeons or like mountain lions attacking sheep or like a forest fire killing everything in its path. None of the men on board Apsyrtus' ship escaped death.

Jason went to the ship, eager to help in the killing, but all of the enemy were already dead. Indeed, the Argonauts were ready to leave to help Jason.

Jason and the Argonauts debated what to do next. Medea joined them. First to come up with a good plan was Peleus, who said, "While it is still dark, we must sail away and hide on an island in the sea east of Italy. In the morning, the enemy will see what has happened. Now that Apsyrtus is dead, I believe that the enemy will no longer — or for not much longer — be concerned with finding and punishing us. Without Apsyrtus as their leader, they will begin to quarrel among themselves and will soon split up into different groups and depart. We can then resume our journey."

They agreed to follow Peleus' plan and sailed away and hid on the Island of Amber.

When the Colchians discovered that Apsyrtus and his men had been murdered, their first thought was to get vengeance for the deaths. But the goddess Hera sent a thunderstorm to delay them, and as they waited for the thunderstorm to stop, they remembered the threats that King Aeetes had made against them. Now that Jason had killed Apsyrtus, King Aeetes would kill them if they returned to Colchis. Therefore, they decided not to return. They split up into various groups, and they traveled in different directions and founded cities in new places.

Jason and the Argonauts set sail again on the *Argo*. Finding the way difficult because of many islets that made sailing dangerous, they stopped for a time and stayed with the Hylleans, who welcomed them. Jason gave the Hylleans a gift: a tripod — one of a pair — that Apollo had given to him when he had consulted the Oracle at Delphi. Enemies would never conquer whatever land one of these tripods was on, and so the Hylleans buried the tripod deep in a secret, hidden spot.

Jason and the Argonauts could not meet King Hyllus because he had died. His parents were Heracles and the water-nymph Melite, and he was born in Phaeacia. Hera hated Heracles and sent him fits of madness, and in one of his fits of madness he had murdered his children — a horrible act. Heracles went to Phaeacia to get help from King Nausithous, who was the King of the Phaeacians. Later, the Trojan War hero Odysseus would visit Phaeacia and see King Alcinous, the son of King Nausithous. King Nausithous was able to help Heracles cleanse himself of his pollution, and Heracles then fell in love with Melite, who gave birth to Hyllus, their son.

After Hyllus had become an adult, he decided to travel. Taking some Phaeacians with him, he founded a city. In this land, he died as he attempted to keep pirates from raiding his cattle.

Jason and the Argonauts had much further to travel. Jason's treacherous murder of Apsyrtus had angered Zeus, who decreed that Jason must expiate the sin with the help of the goddess Circe. In addition, Zeus decreed that Jason and the Argonauts must suffer many hardships before returning home.

Jason and the Argonauts traveled far to the south in the sea east of Italy, and they saw the home of the goddess Calypso, but Hera respected the wishes of her husband, Zeus, and sent a wind that blew the *Argo* back to the Island of Amber.

During the thunderstorm, the beam that the goddess Athena had used in the prow of the *Argo* — the beam came from a tree that had grown in Dodona, where a shrine was dedicated to Zeus, king of gods and mortals — began to speak. The voice told Jason and the Argonauts the punishment that Zeus had decreed for them for the treacherous murder of Apsyrtus: hardships and journeys. The voice also said that Circe would help Jason to expiate the sin of the treacherous murder of Apsyrtus. The voice also ordered Polydeuces and Castor to pray and beg the gods that the *Argo* be allowed to sail to the sea west of Italy and find Circe.

Polydeuces and Castor immediately obeyed the voice of the beam and prayed. Nevertheless, the other Argonauts were unhappy and depressed.

Jason and the Argonauts knew a route that would take them to the sea west of Italy: They could sail up the Eridanus River to where it meets the Rhone River, and then they could sail down the Rhone to where it empties into the sea west of Italy. The *Argo* started to sail up the Eridanus River.

Jason and the Argonauts reached the lake where Phaëton had fallen. Overflow from this lake poured into the Eridanus River. Phaëton had heard that he was the son of Helios the Sun-god, so he journeyed to Helios and asked him whether he, Helios, was his father. Helios replied that yes, he was Phaëton's father. Phaëton asked Helios to give him whatever gift he desired. Helios swore an inviolable oath that he would, and Phaëton said that the gift he wanted was to drive the chariot of the Sun across the sky. Because Helios had sworn an inviolable oath, he had to let Phaëton drive the chariot of the Sun, but Phaëton was unable to control the immortal horses that pulled the chariot. The Sun traveled wildly in the sky, sometimes going far from the Earth and freezing it and sometimes coming close to the Earth and burning it. To prevent the Earth from being destroyed, Zeus threw a lightning bolt that killed Phaëton, who fell into this lake.

The body of Phaëton is still smoldering in the lake and is still making the lake hot. Clouds of steam rise from the lake. Birds that fly into the steam faint and fall into the lake and drown. The Heliades — the Daughters of Helios — whom the gods had turned into poplars, still mourn the death of Phaëton, their brother, and cry tears of amber that the wind blows into the Eridanus River, which washes them downstream.

According to the Celts, however, the amber drops are actually the tears of the god Apollo, shed as he mourned for his mortal son Asclepius, whom Zeus killed because he dared to bring the dead back to life. Zeus temporarily banished Apollo to this area, and Apollo cried tears of amber as he mourned for his dead son.

Jason and the Argonauts could neither eat nor drink because of their nausea from breathing the foul air that came from Phaëton's smoldering corpse. At night, they could not sleep because the Heliades shrieked with grief.

Jason and the Argonauts sailed up the Eridanus River to where it met the Rhone River, and then they sailed down the Rhone River. One branch of the river flows into the Ocean, which circles all land and is deadly to sailors. At one point in their journey, in an area filled with lakes, they nearly sailed into the branch that led to the Ocean. If they had sailed into the Ocean, they never would have survived, but the goddess Hera was watching the *Argo*, and she revealed herself to the Argonauts. She stood on a mountain and shrieked. The Argonauts, terrified, changed their course and sailed until they reached the sea west of Italy. Polydeuces and Castor, who are still known as the saviors of ships, played major roles in keeping the *Argo* safe, and Zeus made them the guardians of many ships that had not then been built. To show their gratitude, people have built many altars and temples to honor Polydeuces and Castor.

After reaching the sea west of Italy, Jason and the Argonauts sailed in search of the goddess Circe, and they found her on the west coast of Italy in a region called Aea, which is also the name of the city ruled by King Aeetes, her brother. She was washing her hair in the sea. She had also washed her clothes in order to purify herself after a terrifying dream she had had during the night. She had dreamed that blood flooded her house and that fire was burning all of her drugs and potions. She had also dreamed that she had scooped up in her hands the blood of a murdered man and put out the fire with the blood. When morning came, she took the steps needed to purify herself.

Jason and the Argonauts stared at Circe, near whom were a number of creatures that were neither human nor animal. Early in the history of the Earth, such creatures arose from chaos. Much time was needed to form human beings and animals.

As Jason and the Argonauts stared at Circe, they noticed a family resemblance to King Aeetes. Both Circe and King Aeetes shared a father: Helios. They were half-brother and half-sister. Circe was immortal; King Aeetes was not.

Now that Circe had purified herself, she was ready to return home, and she invited the Argonauts to go with her. Jason ordered them to stay with the *Argo*, but he and Medea followed Circe and entered her home.

Although Circe was a goddess, she did not know why Jason and Medea were visiting her. She invited them to sit in chairs, but instead they sat on the floor in front of the hearth. Medea hid her face with her hands. Jason stuck his sword — the sword with which he had murdered Apsyrtus — into the dirt floor, and he stared at the floor. Neither Medea nor Jason was willing to look Circe in the eyes. From these actions, Circe knew that Medea and Jason were suppliants — they had committed a murder that Zeus abhorred and so they had come to her so that she could perform rituals to expiate their sin.

Zeus is a god who abhors treacherous murders, and yet Zeus is a god who is willing to forgive a murderer if the murderer performs the proper actions and the proper sacrifices.

Circe knew what needed to be done to expiate a treacherous murder. A pig had recently given birth — her dugs were swollen with milk. Circe took one of the piglets and cut its throat. She let the blood gush out over the hands of Medea and of Jason. She poured libations out to Zeus and prayed to him in his guises as Purifier and as Respecter of Suppliants.

The water-nymphs who served Circe carried impurities out of her house, and she burned cakes and other offerings to Zeus and the Furies. Because the Furies always reject offerings of wine, Circe poured no wine as a sacrifice. Circe wanted to persuade the Furies not to seek vengeance for whatever treacherous murder that Medea and Jason had committed. Circe also wanted Zeus to forgive Medea and Jason for whatever treacherous murder they had committed.

Once Circe had completed the rite and the sacrifices, she raised Medea and Jason up from the floor and made them sit in chairs. She sat and watched their faces as she questioned them. She wanted to know where they had traveled and where they had come from and what murder they had committed.

She remembered her nightmare of the previous night, and she wondered what her kinswoman, Medea, would say. Circe had realized that Medea was her kinswoman from her eyes — the descendants of Helios all have distinctive, flashing eyes. Medea was Circe's niece.

Medea, using the language of her people, answered the questions that Circe asked. She told the story of the Argonauts, of her father's treatment of them, of how her sister had tempted her to help them, and of how she fled with them from her father's wrath. Medea did not, however, tell Circe about the murder of Apsyrtus. Circe was aware of the omission, but she still pitied Medea despite being aware of the need for justice. Because Circe was a sorceress, she guessed — and then knew — that the suppliants had murdered Apsyrtus, Medea's brother and Circe's nephew.

Circe said to Medea, "All that you have done will make for a very unhappy homecoming for you. King Aeetes, I believe, will come for you. Although you have not mentioned the murder of his son, I am aware of it, and I know that

King Aeetes' wrath is terrifying. You have wronged him. You have treacherously murdered his son.

"I myself will not harm you. You are a suppliant, and I am your aunt. However, you must leave my home and my island. This man who is with you must also leave. You have chosen him over your father. And do not kneel before me, do not supplicate me, do not ask me for mercy, because I cannot approve of the actions you have done and the choices you have made. You should not have disobeyed and fled from your father."

Medea grieved. She covered her eyes with her robe and cried. Jason held her hand and led her out of Circe's house. Medea was afraid of what could happen to her.

Hera had ordered Iris, the messenger goddess, to keep watch on Jason and Medea; she wanted to know when they would leave Circe's house and board the *Argo*.

Iris informed Hera that Jason and Medea had left Circe's house, and Hera said to Iris, "I have orders for you. First, find Thetis and tell her to come to me. I have a job for her to do. Second, go to Hephaestus, the blacksmith god, and tell him not to work his bellows until after the *Argo* has passed his workshop. Hephaestus' bellows heat a volcano and melt rock into lava, and I want the *Argo* to pass his workshop safely. Third, go to Aeolus, king of the winds, and tell him to keep his winds locked up — all except a favorable wind that will blow the *Argo* to the island of the Phaeacians."

Iris quickly obeyed. She found Thetis, a sea-nymph, with Nereus, the sea-god who was her father, and told her to go to Hera. She found Hephaestus and relayed Hera's message, and Hephaestus and the Cyclopes who worked for him immediately stopped melting metal and working with hammers and anvils. Finally, Iris delivered Hera's message to Aeolus, king of the winds.

Thetis left Nereus and her sister sea-nymphs and flew to Olympus to see Hera, who gave her a seat and then said, "Thetis, I want to keep Jason and the Argonauts safe. Earlier, Athena kept them safe as they sailed through the Clashing Rocks. I want to make sure that they are safe when they soon sail through the Wandering Rocks. They will also face the challenge of sailing between the man-eating monster Scylla, who lives in a cave in a cliff, and the whirlpool that is called Charybdis.

"You know that I respect and love you. In fact, I helped to raise you. When you were grown, my husband, Zeus, tried to sleep with you, as he does so often with beautiful goddesses and beautiful mortal women. You resisted his advances out of your respect of me — and fear of the consequences of sleeping with my husband. You resisted his advances even though he punished you by taking an inviolable oath that you would never marry a god. Even after you successfully resisted him, he still felt sexual desire for you — until Themis, the goddess of justice, told him of your destiny. She told him that you were destined to give birth to a son who would be greater than his father. After hearing that, Zeus no longer wanted to sleep with you because he did not want you to give birth to a son who would grow to adulthood and take Zeus' place as king of gods and men. Zeus wishes to be the king of gods and men forever.

"I chose a mortal husband for you. I chose Peleus because I wanted you to be a happy wife and mother. Peleus is a hero — he is one of the Argonauts. I carried the bridal torch at your wedding, to which I had invited gods and goddesses. You gave birth to Achilles, who will be a greater hero than his father. Chiron the Centaur is now raising Achilles. Although you are his mother, you do not feed Achilles with milk from your breasts; water-nymphs feed him.

"Now I will tell you something new about your son, Achilles. He is mortal, and after he dies, he will go to the happy part of the Land of the Dead: the Elysium Fields. There, he will marry Medea, one of the daughters of King Aeetes. You are Medea's future mother-in-law, and I want you to help Medea now. I also want you to help Peleus. Although he is a hero, he did something foolish and angered you and so you left him. These things happen. The goddess Ate makes men — and even gods — sometimes behave foolishly. Ate is the goddess of delusion and ruin.

"I have already sent a message to Hephaestus and to Aeolus to ask for their help for Medea and Peleus. I have no doubt that they will do what I have requested. Hephaestus will keep his blacksmith fires low so that the *Argo* can safely pass by, and Aeolus will send only a favorable breeze so that the *Argo* can safely reach the island of the Phaeacians.

"I also want you to help Jason and the Argonauts. Some challenges lie ahead for them that I want you and your sister sea-nymphs to help them through. The Wandering Rocks are one challenge. Scylla and Charybdis are another challenge. Do not let the *Argo* go too close to Charybdis or the whirlpool will suck down the ship and drown all on board. But do not let the *Argo* go too close to Scylla — whose mother is Hecate — or the monster will reach out with her six heads and long necks and seize and devour — alive — as many people on board the *Argo* as she can. I want you to save the Argonauts — keep the ship in the exact center where those on board will be safe."

Thetis replied, "I will do as you wish, and as long as Hephaestus' fires are low and Aeolus' wind is favorable, I and my sisters will be successful in helping Jason and the Argonauts. But I have much to do: I need to see my sisters and recruit their help, and I need to go to the *Argo* and tell the Argonauts that they should leave at dawn if they want to see their homeland again."

Thetis flew to the sea and called her sisters to come to her. She sent them to the Wandering Rocks to wait to help the *Argo*, and then she went to Aea to see her estranged husband, Peleus.

She approached Peleus and held his hand. Other Argonauts were nearby, but only her husband saw her. She said to him, "You and the Argonauts have been here long enough; it is time for all of you to set sail again. Hera herself wishes you to leave at dawn. She has ordered my sister sea-nymphs and me to keep the Argonauts safe and to help the *Argo* get safely through the Wandering Rocks. You will see my sisters and me when the *Argo* reaches the Wandering Rocks. When that happens, do not tell any of the Argonauts that you have seen me. If you do, I will be even angrier at you than I was when I left you and my son." Thetis then dived into the sea.

Peleus grieved. He had not seen Thetis since she became angry at him and left him. He had not understood what Thetis was doing when he woke up early and saw her put their son, Achilles, in the fire in their hearth. Achilles gasped in the flames, and Peleus cried out in alarm. Thetis snatched Achilles from the fire and dropped him on the floor in front of the fire. Later, Peleus understood that Thetis had been in the process of making Achilles immortal so that he need never grow old. Each day, she anointed Achilles with ambrosia, the food of the immortal gods; each night, she put Achilles in the fire. If Peleus had not interrupted the process, his son would have become a god. He regretted thinking that Thetis had ill intentions toward Achilles. He knew now that Thetis loved Achilles, but Thetis would never return and act as his wife again.

Peleus told Jason and the Argonauts what Thetis had told him. They agreed to leave at dawn. In the morning, they left. A favorable wind filled the sails of the *Argo*.

Soon, they reached the island of the Sirens, whose mother had been the muse Terpsichore. The Sirens were part bird and part human female. They sang, and the beauty of their singing led sailors to forget their homecoming and instead stay with the Sirens and listen to their songs while forgetting to eat and slowly starving to death.

Orpheus realized the danger that the Argonauts were in, and so he started to play his lyre and sing in competition with the Sirens. His song was loud and lively, and it mostly drowned out the song of the Sirens. The current and the wind swept the *Argo* past the Sirens. Only one Argonaut — Butes, who loved battle — jumped overboard to swim to the Sirens. The goddess Aphrodite felt pity for him and rescued him and set him on shore far from the Sirens.

More challenges lay ahead for the Argonauts. They were close to Scylla and Charybdis. Thetis, unseen by the Argonauts, swam behind the *Argo*, grabbed the steering oar, and kept the *Argo* in the safe passage exactly in between Scylla and Charybdis. No Argonauts were harmed.

Past Scylla and Charybdis were the Wandering Rocks in a narrow place where two great bodies of water meet. Hephaestus' workshop usually filled the air around the Wandering Rocks with steam and smoke. Earlier, flames could have been seen shooting up from lava, but Hephaestus had obeyed Hera and stopped his bellows and ceased his work.

The Nereids — the daughters of the sea-god Nereus who were Thetis' sisters — were waiting for the *Argo*. Thetis continued to guide the *Argo* with the steering oar, and the Nereids, like a school of dolphins, swam around the *Argo* until it reached the Wandering Rocks. Then the Nereids tied their skirts above their knees to keep them out of the way and ran on top of the water alongside the *Argo* and kept it on a safe course although the current tried to make it go right or left. The Wandering Rocks sometimes rose up like a mountain and sometimes were swallowed by the water. Nereids grabbed the sides of the *Argo* and pushed it forward. They were like young girls playing a game on a beach. The Nereids kept the *Argo* away from the dangerous Wandering Rocks as Hephaestus watched as he stood on a volcano with his hammer beside him. His hammer was so huge that he rested his shoulder on its handle. Also watching were the goddesses Hera and Athena; Hera was terrified that the Argonauts would die and so she hugged Athena for reassurance.

It was hard work, but Thetis and the other Nereids got the *Argo* through the Wandering Rocks with no loss of life. The wind filled the sails of the *Argo* as it sailed to the island of the sheep and cattle of the Sun. Here the Nereids left the *Argo* and dived into the sea.

On the island two daughters of Helios — Phaëthusa and Lampetie — took care of their father's animals. The cows were white and had golden horns. The Argonauts could hear the bleating of the sheep and the lowing of the cows as they passed the island.

At dawn, they reached the island of the Phaeacians, under whose earth is said to lie the sickle that the god Cronos had used to castrate his father, Uranus, who had treated his wife, Gaia, badly and imprisoned their children. However, other people thought that Demeter, goddess of the harvest, had used the sickle. She had once lived on the island and taught the inhabitants — the Titans — how to use sickles to harvest grain. Demeter had done this out of her respect for Makris, the nurse of Dionysus. After being driven away from the island of Euboea, Makris lived on this island — the island of the Phaeacians.

Ruling the Phaeacians were King Alcinous and Queen Arete, who welcomed Jason and the Argonauts, as did all the Phaeacians. Jason and the Argonauts felt as happy as if they had reached their own homes. But soon, trouble arose.

Some of the Colchians had sailed out of the Black Sea and through the Clashing Rocks in search of Jason and the Argonauts. That fleet of ships showed up at the island of the Phaeacians. The Colchian leaders demanded that Medea be given to them so that they could return her to her father, King Aeetes. They declared that they would attack the Phaeacians unless they received Medea, and then they threatened that King Aeetes would soon arrive with more ships and also attack the Phaeacians.

A good man, King Alcinous asked for time in which to make a decision. He did not want fighting and blood and death. He wanted a peaceful and fair resolution to the conflict.

Medea was terrified that she would be handed over to the Colchians. She begged the Argonauts and, separately, Queen Arete, not to allow that to happen.

Medea kneeled before Queen Arete and held her knees and begged her, "I am your guest and your supplicant, and I plead with you not to allow the Colchians to take me back to King Aeetes, my father. You are a woman like me, and you know that one misdeed can lead to another. I disobeyed the wishes of my stern and strict father and helped Jason and the Argonauts stay alive. I did it out of pity and to help my cousins — the four sons of my sister. I did not intend to run away with Jason and the Argonauts, but I realized that the consequences of disobeying my father's wishes would be severe. Avoiding that punishment was my motive for running away from my father.

"I did not disobey my father's wishes out of lust. I am still a virgin — I swear that by the Sun who loves the light and by Hecate who loves the dark.

"Pity me, and help me. Talk to your husband the king and convince him not to send me back to my father.

"I wish for you only the best: respect from other people, children, and peace on your island."

Queen Arete would get the children that Medea wished for her. Among her children would be a daughter named Nausicaa, who would give the Trojan War hero Odysseus help when he greatly needed it.

That was how Medea begged Queen Arete for mercy. When pleading with the Argonauts, Medea used other appeals. She talked to each of the Argonauts separately and said, "I helped you, and because I helped you, I am in trouble with my father. Because of my help, Jason was able to yoke the bulls, plow the field of Ares, plant the teeth of the dragon, and kill the warriors who grew from the earth. Because I helped you, you now have the Golden Fleece and are alive and are sailing back to your homes. Because I helped you, I have lost my home and my parents. You still have a home — I do not!

"Remember that you promised to protect me — you swore an oath! Respect me, a supplant! What will happen to you if I am given back to my father and he kills me! What will the gods do to you if you do not keep your oath to protect me! The Furies punish those who break oaths and do not respect suppliants.

"I am not seeking help in a temple. I am seeking help from you, but you do not seem to be willing to help me. At one time, you were brave — when you wanted the Golden Fleece. But now that you have the Golden Fleece, you do not seem to be willing to help me."

Each of the Argonauts tried to reassure her that he would protect her. Each showed her his sword and his spear and promised to fight if she did not receive a just decision from King Alcinous.

That night, the Argonauts slept, but Medea did not. She cried; she was afraid. She was like a woman crying as she spins yarn at night to support her children now that she is their lone support because her husband has died. The woman mourns her hard, unhappy life.

King Alcinous and Queen Arete discussed Medea that night as they lay in bed side by side.

Queen Arete said to her husband, "Darling, have mercy on Medea and protect her. It is better to side with the Thessalians than with the Colchians. Thessaly is much closer to us than Colchis is. We have heard the name of King Aeetes, but we have never seen him.

"I pity Medea, who has made a personal appeal to me. Please do not let the Colchians take her back to her father, King Aeetes. Besides, Medea made a mistake, but she knows she made a mistake. She should have obeyed the wishes of her father and been a dutiful daughter, but she instead helped Jason avoid death. Once she had made that mistake, its consequences led to her making another mistake. That is something that happens to very many humans. Once she had helped Jason, she feared her father and so decided to run away from him by sailing on the *Argo* with Jason and the Argonauts.

"Jason has promised her that he will marry her and make her his own, legally wedded wife. Darling, you ought not to cause Jason to break his oath. Also, darling, you ought not to allow King Aeetes to do something dreadful to his daughter Medea. Fathers can be overly strict and overly demanding.

"Remember Nycteus and his daughter Antiope. She became pregnant by Zeus, who had taken the form of a satyr, and she fled from her father, Nycteus, who had threatened her. Nycteus committed suicide.

"Remember Danaë. Her father, Acrisius, heard a prophecy that her son would kill him, so he kept her shut away from men so that she would not become pregnant. Zeus, however, came to her in the form of golden rain and made her pregnant. Her father put her and her son, whose name was Perseus, in a chest and threw it into the sea. It washed ashore on an island. Much later, Perseus participated in athletic games and accidentally killed an old man with a wild throw of a javelin. That old man was Acrisius.

"Remember cruel Echetus, who lives not far from us. Recently, he discovered that his daughter was involved in a love affair. He punished her by driving spikes into her eyes and blinding her. He continues to punish her by making her grind metal as if she were grinding grain into flour."

King Alcinous, who loved his wife, replied, "Arete, if need be, I could with my warriors defeat the Colchians in order to help Medea, but I must do the right thing. Zeus wishes daughters to be dutiful, and Medea has not been a dutiful daughter. At the same time, Zeus wishes wives to be loyal to their husbands. I need to do what Zeus wishes me to do. In addition, I must do what is best for our people. King Aeetes may rule a land that is far away, but he is a powerful king, and if he wishes, he can make war against civilizations in Greece. As King of the Phaeacians, I must make a just decision concerning Medea — a decision that all will agree is the best decision.

"Let me tell you what I have decided. If Medea is still an unmarried virgin, I will rule that she be taken back to her father, King Aeetes. But if Medea is a married woman, I will rule that she stay with her husband. And if Medea is pregnant, I will rule that the baby she will give birth to will stay with her and her husband."

King Alcinous fell asleep, but Queen Arete got out of bed and sought her herald. She told him to take a message to Jason: He must marry Medea at once. That way, King Alcinous would rule that Medea must stay with Jason. But if Medea and Jason would not marry immediately, King Alcinous would rule that Medea be sent back to her father, King Aeetes.

The herald left the palace and found Jason and told him the news. Jason and the Argonauts were happy to hear the herald's message, and they immediately prepared the wedding.

They mixed wine for the gods and sacrificed sheep to the gods, and they prepared Medea's bridal bed in the cave that had once been the home of Macris. The father of Macris was Aristaeus, who loved honey and discovered the arts of bee-keeping and growing olive trees. Macris was the nurse of Dionysus, whose mother, Semele, died. After Zeus made Semele pregnant with Dionysus, Hera, who hated her husband's affairs, visited Semele and made her doubt that Zeus was really the father of her fetus. Therefore, Semele made Zeus swear an inviolable oath that he would give her something she wanted. He did, and Semele said that she wanted Zeus to reveal himself to her in his full glory. Zeus, who knew what would happen, did not want to do this — the gods do not appear in their full glory to humans for good reason — but Semele insisted. Because the oath Zeus had sworn was inviolable, he appeared before her in his full glory and the sight incinerated her. But Hermes rescued from the flames the fetus she was carrying and gave it to Zeus, who sewed it into his thigh from which it was born. Because of this, Dionysus was known as the twice-born — both Semele and Zeus had carried him as a fetus. Because Dionysus had been fathered by Zeus and born from Zeus' thigh, he became an immortal god. Hermes then took the infant to the island of Euboea, where Macris nursed the infant and fed it honey. Hera disliked her husband's affairs and she often hated the children who were the result of those affairs, so she forced Makris to leave the island of Euboea. Makris settled on the island of the Phaeacians. She made a cave her home, and she made the Phaeacians prosperous.

In the cave of Makris, the Argonauts prepared Medea's bridal bed. On it they spread the Golden Fleece. Nymphs of streams and mountains and woods gathered armfuls of flowers of different colors and brought them into the cave, and the Golden Fleece reflected light onto the nymphs. The nymphs wanted to touch the Golden Fleece, but they were afraid to fulfill their desire. Hera had sent the nymphs to the wedding to honor Jason.

During the wedding, the Argonauts held spears in case of an attack of the Colchians. Armed, the Argonauts sang the wedding hymns while Orpheus played his lyre. At the wedding, the nymphs sang and danced. They sang and danced to honor Hera, who had put into the mind of Queen Arete the idea to tell Jason to immediately marry Medea.

And so Jason and Medea were married on the island of the Phaeacians although Jason and Medea had wanted the marriage to take place in his father's house in Thessaly.

Human beings can never be completely happy, and although Jason and Medea were happy, they still worried that something could go wrong and Medea could be forced to go back to her father.

The next morning, everyone arose, and King Alcinous went to the Colchians to tell them what he had decided in the case of Medea. He carried a judge's golden staff — the staff he always carried when giving his fair and impartial decisions. The Phaeacians and the Argonauts went with him. News that the decision would be made spread to all, and gossip — started by Hera

— spread that Jason and Medea were married. A wedding meant that this would be a festive day. One man brought a ram. Another man brought a heifer. Women brought appropriate gifts for a bride: gold jewelry and embroidered robes. The good looks of the Argonauts impressed the women. Orpheus sang a song about the wedding, and the nymphs danced. The smoke of sacrifices filled the air.

The Colchians protested against King Alcinous' decision that since Medea was a married woman, she must stay with her husband and not with her father. But King Alcinous did not allow their protests to change his mind. He was sure that he had made the right and just decision, and because of that, he was not afraid of King Aeetes. King Alcinous had made the Colchians and the Argonauts swear oaths that they would abide by his decision. King Alcinous also threatened that he would never allow any Colchians to use the Phaeacians' harbors if they did not accept his decision. He told the Colchians that they must either accept his decision or immediately sail away. When the Colchians realized that King Alcinous had many warriors and that he would not change his mind, they grew worried about what King Aeetes would do to them if they returned to Colchis without Medea — he had stated that the penalty for not bringing Medea back was death — and so they asked King Alcinous for sanctuary. King Alcinous granted their request, and for a long time, the Colchians lived on the island of the Phaeacians, with whom they became friends.

After spending seven days on the island of the Phaeacians, the Argonauts left. Both King Alcinous and Queen Arete gave them many gifts — Queen Arete gave Medea twelve Phaeacian young women to be her servants.

Zeus sent a favorable wind to the *Argo*, and the Argonauts set sail, but they still had troubles to face and problems to solve.

The waters around Libya were dangerous. A storm wind from the north drove the *Argo* into the gulf of Syrtis off Libya. This gulf is deadly to ships, and once they enter they cannot leave. The gulf is filled with dangerous rocks and seaweed and areas of shallow water. Also, the winds always blow into the gulf and never out of the gulf, and the currents made rowing out of the gulf impossible. The land of Libya is also dangerous: hot sand and little or no water. Few animals except poisonous snakes and their prey can live there. Even worse, the storm waves and an incoming tide had combined to lift the *Argo* high and drop it onto the Libyan shore.

The Argonauts got onto shore and surveyed their situation. Even if they got the *Argo* back into the water, they would not be able to safely navigate out of the gulf, and the land itself was inhospitable. They saw no drinking water, no paths or roads, and no inhabitants or homes. They saw only a silent, lifeless desert. They saw no birds or animals.

The Argonauts now wished that they had taken the same route home that they had taken to get to the Black Sea — even if that had meant disobeying the will of Zeus. If they had done that, they would probably be dead, but they felt that was preferable to being where they now were.

The Argonauts looked at the gulf and at the desert and wondered how they could survive for even a few days.

Ancaeus, the pilot of the *Argo*, despaired. He said, "We can never get out of this gulf. Shallows and rocks are everywhere. The *Argo* would have been smashed to pieces long ago except that high waves and a flood tide lifted it over the rocks. Now that the high waves and flood tide are ebbing, the *Argo* is stranded on shore. Even if it were in the water, it would not be able to sail — there is not enough water to keep the ship from hitting bottom. Even when there is another flood tide, the winds and currents will prevent the *Argo* from leaving the gulf. We are forced to give up our hopes of ever returning home.

"If anyone knows how we can get the *Argo* out of this gulf, let him take over as pilot. As for myself, I do not believe that Zeus intends for any of us to return home."

All of the Argonauts who understood the art of sailing also despaired. No one knew how to get the *Argo* out of the gulf.

Jason and the Argonauts seemed doomed, and they believed that they were doomed, and so they gave up. They said their goodbyes to each other, and then each wandered hopelessly to find a lonely spot to die. They wandered like men who are hopeless because of bad omens: statues weeping bloody tears, sounds of bellowing coming from empty temples, and stars appearing at noon as the Sun hides. They were like hopeless men expecting war, or plague, or the devastation of their crops by floods.

That night, they wrapped their heads in their cloaks and lay on the sand. All that night and long into the following day, they waited to die. They did not eat or drink.

Medea and her servants also mourned. They lay with their hair in the dust and cried out in grief. They sounded like birds that cannot fly and that chirp for their mother when they fall out of the nest. They sounded as mournful as the echo of swans singing on a river during a misty morning.

All of them could have died there and been forgotten and been left out of heroic songs. But nymphs — the protectors of Libya — saw them and pitied them. These nymphs had assisted Athena. Zeus lusted after Metis, goddess of wisdom, and he got her pregnant. But Zeus heard a prophecy about the children of Metis: Her first child would be a girl, but her second child would be a boy who, when grown, would overthrow his father. Zeus did not want to be overthrown, so he swallowed Metis, who then made — inside Zeus — armor for her daughter. Zeus got a headache one day, and he instructed Hephaestus to get an axe and hit him on the head with it. (Being immortal, Zeus knew that he would not die.) After Hephaestus split open Zeus' skull, the fully grown, fully armed goddess Athena sprang out. Athena became the goddess of wisdom. The nymphs of Libya bathed Athena after she was born from Zeus' head.

At noon, when the Sun was blazingly hot in the Libyan desert, the nymphs went to Jason and gently removed the cloak that was covering his head. Jason immediately realized that they were goddesses, and he lowered his eyes out of respect for them.

The nymphs said to Jason, "Why are you and the Argonauts despairing? Are you not the men who acquired the Golden Fleece? We know about that heroic deed and about all of the other deeds that you and the Argonauts have performed. We are the guardians of Libya, and we are immortal. Get up, and make your men get up. And remember what we say to you now: Amphitrite — the wife of Poseidon, god of the sea — will unyoke his horses. When that happens, you must repay your mother — she carried you a long time in her womb despite suffering pain. After you repay your mother, you can return home."

When the nymphs had finished speaking to Jason, they disappeared. Jason prayed, "Guardians of Libya, I will do as you tell me to do. I will gather the Argonauts and Medea and her servants and tell them what you have told me.

I do not understand the meaning of your words, but perhaps one of the others will."

Covered with dust from the sand in the desert, Jason stood up and yelled for the others to gather around him. He was like a yellow lion that roars for its mate — the lion frightens herdsmen and makes mountains tremble. But Jason's voice was welcome to the Argonauts. Jason, his men, and Medea and her women all gathered near the *Argo*.

Jason said to them, "Three goddesses — the protectors of Libya — just now came to me. They were dressed like young Libyan women in goatskin dresses. They told me to gather all of you. They also told me that Amphitrite — the wife of Poseidon, god of the sea — will unyoke his horses. They added that when that happens, we must repay our mother — she carried us a long time in her womb despite suffering pain. That is the oracle the goddesses gave to me, but I do not understand it. The three goddesses know all about our adventures. When they had finished speaking to me, they disappeared."

Almost immediately, a huge horse came out of the sea. It shook itself, and then it galloped across the desert.

Peleus interpreted the oracle: "Clearly, this is the horse of the sea-god Poseidon — this horse came out of the sea. Poseidon's wife has unyoked it. That part of the oracle is clear enough, but I can also interpret the other part. The mother in whose womb we have been carried is the *Argo* — the ship in which we have been carried over the sea. The *Argo*'s timbers have often groaned as the ship carried us. Now we can repay the *Argo*. She carried us — now we will carry her! We will follow the tracks of Poseidon's horse. Because it is the horse of a sea-god, it will seek the sea. It has left this gulf and is now running over the desert to a body of water that either is the sea or will take us to the sea."

Jason and the Argonauts agreed that Peleus had interpreted the oracle correctly: They would carry the *Argo* across the desert.

For over a week, they did just that. They lifted the *Argo* and carried it shoulder high across the sand dunes of Libya. This cost them much pain and much misery, but they were the sons and grandsons of gods and they did not give up. The tracks of the horse led them to a lagoon, and they placed the *Argo* in the lagoon's salty water.

And now they looked for fresh water with which to quench their thirst. They were like mad dogs, but they were mad with thirst.

They found help. They found the Hesperides, three goddesses in whose garden grows a tree whose fruit is golden apples. The serpent named Ladon guarded the tree, but the serpent was dead — Heracles had killed it. The tail of the serpent twitched, but the rest of it was motionless. Heracles had shot the serpent with his arrows whose tips had been dipped in the poisonous blood of the monster known as the Hydra. The serpent's festering wounds attracted flies, and they died in the wounds. Heracles had also taken the tree's golden apples, causing the Hesperides to mourn.

The Hesperides were mourning as the Argonauts suddenly appeared before them. Immediately, the Hesperides turned to dust at the feet of the Argonauts.

Orpheus prayed to them: "Goddesses, have mercy on us and appear before us. Tell us where to find water, whether it comes from a spring in the ground or from a spring flowing from the rocks of a hillside. Let us quench our thirst, or we will die. If we survive and make it home, we will treat you as we treat the very greatest goddesses — we will sacrifice to you and pour out libations for you."

As Orpheus prayed, he wept. The Hesperides heard his prayer, and they decided to answer it. At the feet of the Argonauts, three shoots came up out of the sand and grew until they were fully mature trees. Hespere was a poplar, Erytheis was an elm, and Aegle was a willow. When the trees became fully grown, they turned into the three goddesses again.

Aegle said to the Argonauts, "We have not been fortunate, but you have been. Yesterday, a cruel man came to our garden. He killed our snake that guarded the tree with the golden apples, and he stole our golden apples. He brought suffering to us, but he also brought release from suffering to you.

"The man was a cruel brute who wore the skin of a lion and who carried a huge club. He also carried a bow and poisoned arrows with which he killed our snake. Like you, he came on foot across the desert, and he had run out of water. He sought water here, but he could not find any. But then — whether it was his own idea or a god put the idea in his head — he kicked a rocky hillside and water poured out from the side of the hillside. He got down on his hands and knees and drank the water thirstily like a dog or other beast."

Aegle pointed to where Heracles — for it was he who had stolen the golden apples from the Hesperides — had created the spring. The Argonauts and the women crowded around the water and drank. They were like many ants trying to get to the tiny hole that leads to their nest. They were like flies landing on a tiny drop of honey and trying to eat their fill while other flies also try to land on the tiny drop of honey.

After all had finally quenched their thirst, and all had water moistening their lips, Jason and the Argonauts spoke about Heracles and how he had saved them from a thirsty death.

One of the Argonauts suggested that they should try to find Heracles, who was still on foot. Perhaps he had not gone so far that they would be unable to find him.

Five men set off in various directions to try to find Heracles. Zetes and Calaïs, the sons of the North Wind, set off, flying with their winged feet. Euphemus, the fastest man on Earth, ran off in another direction. Lynceus set off in yet another direction, hoping to be able to use his fine eyesight to find Heracles, even if Heracles should be a great distance away. Finally, Canthus set off to find Heracles. He hoped to ask Heracles what had happened to Polyphemus, who was a close friend to Canthus. Heracles and Polyphemus had searched for Hylas, Heracles' companion and armor keeper, and they had accidentally been left behind by the Argonauts. But Polyphemus was dead. He had founded a city and then decided to search for the *Argo* so that he could return to his original home in Greece. During his journey, he was killed. A monument stands to honor him.

Lynceus, whose eyesight was so good that people thought that he could see items that had been buried in the ground, believed that he saw Heracles a great distance away. Lynceus was like a man who believes that he sees the Moon through a mist of cloud. He returned to Jason and the Argonauts and told them that Heracles was so far away that they would be unable to catch up with him.

Euphemus, Zetes, and Calaïs returned to the Argonauts and reported that they had been unable to find Heracles.

Canthus, however, did not return — alive. He had discovered a herd of sheep and was driving it to the camp of the Argonauts, who now had water but no food, so that they could eat. But the shepherd, who was named Caphaurus, followed him, waited for an opportunity, and threw a rock at him and killed him. Caphaurus' grandfather was the god Apollo; Caphaurus' other ancestors included important men in Crete and in Libya. When Jason and the Argonauts discovered that Caphaurus had killed Canthus, they killed Caphaurus and carried Canthus' body and drove Caphaurus' sheep back to their camp, where they buried Canthus.

On the day that the Argonauts buried Canthus, they also buried Mopsus. Although Mopsus was a seer, he was not able to save himself from dying — no man, however wise, can do that. A poisonous snake lay in the sand in the shade cast by a rock. Because of the great heat, it was sluggish and not a danger to any man it did not feel threatened by. But Mopsus had the misfortune to step over the rock and onto the tail of the snake, which bit him. One drop of the venom of the snake was enough to ensure death — not even Paeëon, the physician of the Olympian gods, would have been able to save the life of Mopsus after the snake had bit him.

When Perseus had killed the Gorgon Medusa, who had snakes for hair and who turned to stone any man who looked at her — Perseus had cut her head off while looking at her reflection in his highly polished shield — he had used his winged sandals to fly over the sands of the Libyan desert. Drops of Medusa's blood had dropped onto the desert sand, and each drop of blood had turned into one of the poisonous snakes of the species that killed Mopsus.

Mopsus' snake wound horrified Medea and her female servants, but the wound was not painful. Nevertheless, Mopsus was doomed to die. He began to feel numb, and he slowly lost his sight. He soon died. After his death, the snake's poison caused his flesh to quickly rot and his hair to fall out. The Argonauts quickly dug for him a deep grave. The men and women gave him full honors: They tore their hair, and they marched three times around the grave and then they built a mound over it.

Jason and the Argonauts boarded the *Argo* and searched for a way out of the lagoon. They were in deep water, but a ring of rocks prevented them from reaching open sea. There seemed to be no way out of the lagoon as the *Argo* sailed here and there in the lagoon for an entire day. The *Argo* was like an angry snake slithering in the sand of a desert and searching for a narrow cleft in a rocky cliff into which it can disappear and be safe from the deadly heat of the Sun.

Orpheus suggested giving to the god of the lagoon the other tripod that Apollo had given to Jason — Jason had given the first tripod to the Hylleans as a thank-you gift for their hospitality. The tripod would be a gift in exchange for information about how to row or sail out of the lagoon. All agreed, and they went on shore and set up the tripod that had been a gift from Apollo.

The sea-god Triton, disguised as a young man, appeared before them. He picked up a clod of earth from the shore and said to Euphemus, "Because I have nothing else to offer you as a gift, let me offer you this clod of earth. I want to be your friend. Perhaps I can be your guide and give you information. My father is the god Poseidon, and I am very familiar with this lagoon and with the land here. My name is Eurypylus, and I was born and raised here in Libya."

Euphemus, whose father was Poseidon, gladly accepted the gift of the clod of earth — and the gift of friendship — and said, "We need your help. Against our will, we were driven into the gulf of Syrtis and we could not row or sail out of it. We lifted our ship and carried it across the desert and brought it to the water here. But we are still trapped. We do not know the way — if there is one — out of this lagoon. The rocks are preventing us from reaching the open sea. If you can, please tell us how to leave the lagoon and how to reach Greece."

Triton, still in disguise as a young man, pointed to the mouth of the lagoon and said, "There you will find a narrow opening through which you can row and reach the sea. Look closely. The water is smooth at the mouth of the lagoon, while on either side of the opening the waters are white with foam as they hit the rocks. Row through the opening, and as you sail keep the land on your right and keep sailing northward and eastward until the land falls away from you and goes south. When that happens, sail north and you will reach Crete. Some of the labor will be difficult, but you are young, and young men ought not to object to hard work."

The Argonauts rowed away at once, leaving the tripod behind. Triton, still in disguise as a young man, picked up the tripod and carried it into the water as the Argonauts headed for the mouth of the lagoon. One of the Argonauts looked back and saw that the young man and the tripod had disappeared — no mortal could have carried away the tripod in that short length of time. They rejoiced because they knew that the young man had been a disguised god. They urged Jason to sacrifice their best sheep to the god and to pray to the god. Jason picked up a sheep, held it over the stern, and cut its throat and dropped it into the sea as he prayed, "Sea-god, whether you are called Triton or Phorcys or Nereus, please give us the homecoming that we desire."

Triton emerged from the sea and swam at the bow — the most forward part — of the *Argo*. He was no longer in disguise but appeared as he really was: his top half was like an adult human man while his bottom half was like a sea creature with a forked tail. Triton guided the *Argo* to the mouth of the lagoon. He was like a man leading a racehorse to a competition. The man grasps the mane of the horse, which tosses its head and is eager to gallop.

When the *Argo* came to the open sea, Triton gave it a push with his mighty hand to send it on its way. He then dived deep into the sea. Excited, the Argonauts shouted.

They sailed for a while, and then they stopped for the rest of the day and for that night. At dawn, they set sail and when the wind died, they rowed. They then began crossing the sea north to the island of Crete.

When they reached Crete, they attempted to pull into the harbor of Dicte, but Talos, a giant made of bronze, stopped them. Talos was the last of the men of the Age of Bronze; he was from the generation before that of Jason and the Argonauts. Talos' job was to protect Europa, after whom Europe is named. Zeus abducted Europa after the god assumed the form of a white bull. She got on his back, and he swam with her to Crete, and she became the island's first queen. Zeus gave her Talos to be her protector. Talos circled Crete three times each day looking for and driving away pirates and other invaders. He was invulnerable except at one point of his body. A blood-red vein, covered only by a thin layer of skin, was in his ankle. An injury to that vein could kill him through loss of blood.

Talos threw huge rocks at the *Argo* and he terrified the Argonauts — they quickly backed water to get away from him. They needed to land on Crete to get water and to eat, but they would have sailed away from Crete except that Medea helped them.

Medea said to Jason and the Argonauts, "I can defeat Talos unless his bronze body is immortal. All you need to do is to keep the *Argo* far enough away from him that the huge rocks he throws won't hit the ship. I will use witchcraft to kill him."

The Argonauts kept the *Argo* out of range of the huge rocks, and Jason led Medea — her face covered by her cloak — to the ship's deck. Medea kneeled in supplication and invoked the Spirits of Death that come like hounds out of the Land of the Dead to seek the souls of living men. She sang to them three times, and she prayed to them three times. She sent evil thoughts to Talos, and he thought of death.

Although Medea was not near Talos, she killed him with her deadly thoughts. While he lifted heavy rocks to throw at the *Argo*, he cut his blood-red vein on a sharp rock and his blood poured out of his body. He stood at the top of a cliff, but he grew weak as he lost his blood and he fell from the cliff the way that a tree — only half-felled when the woodman goes home at night — is toppled by the wind during the night and falls down the hillside.

Jason and the Argonauts camped on shore that night, and in the morning they built an altar to Athena before continuing their journey.

Unfortunately, as they sailed at night after leaving Crete they experienced the Deadly Darkness. All was dark on the sea. No Moon shone. No stars were visible. No lights on any land could be seen. For all that Jason and the Argonauts knew, they could have been sailing straight into the Land of the Dead.

Jason lifted his hands to the sky and prayed to Apollo. He wept as he prayed for the *Argo* and his shipmates to be saved. He promised Apollo splendid sacrifices at his most important shrines — the ones at Delphi, at Amyclae near Sparta, and on the island of Delos.

Apollo heard and answered the prayer. He flew down from Mount Olympus and stood on a rock that jutted from the sea. Then he lifted his golden bow, which shot forth beams of golden light by which Jason and the Argonauts could see.

Jason and the Argonauts saw an island that the gleam of Apollo's bow revealed to them, and they anchored there. In the morning, they built an altar to Apollo, whom they called the Lord of Light because he had saved them by providing light. Jason and the Argonauts sacrificed to Apollo what they could, which — at the time — was very little. They had no wine, so they used water when they poured out libations to Apollo.

The young Phaeacian women who served Medea laughed when they saw them pouring out water as a libation. On their home island, they were accustomed to seeing splendid sacrifices of much wine and many animals. The men, happy to be alive, responded to the women with risqué jokes, and the men and women humorously insulted each other and laughed. The women of the island continued this practice of jokingly mocking the men during sacrifices in later years.

At dawn the following morning, they sailed onward. Euphemus, the fastest man in the world, had had a dream during the night. Hermes, the god of dreams, sometimes sends significant dreams, and Euphemus did his best to remember his dream.

The god Triton had given Euphemus a clod of earth when the Argonauts were trying to find a way out of the lagoon in Libya. Euphemus dreamed that he suckled the clod of earth with milk from his nipples. The clod then grew into a young woman who was a virgin. Overcome by desire, Euphemus slept with her and took her virginity. He then felt sad because he had taken her virginity, but the young woman told him, "I am a daughter of Triton and Libya, and I am the nurse of your children. If you give me a home in the sea along with the sea-nymphs who are the daughters of Nereus, I will welcome your children."

Euphemus told his dream to Jason, who interpreted it with the aid of an oracle that he had heard while at Delphi: "This is a positive dream. Throw this clod of earth into the sea, and through the power of the gods it will become an island. Your descendants will come to the island and live there. This is what Triton meant to happen when he gave you this clod of earth as a gift."

Euphemus threw the clod of earth into the sea, and the gods caused an island to rise out of the sea there. The island is named Calliste, and it nursed Euphemus' descendants after Euphemus died.

Jason and the Argonauts now sailed to the island of Aegina, whose king was the father of Peleus and Telamon, who had been exiled from Aegina after killing their half-brother, Phocus. They landed because they needed water, but because all of them wished to sail quickly to Iolcus, they raced as they hauled buckets of water to the *Argo*, making it a game and a competition.

From Aegina to Iolcus, all was easy sailing. No storms occurred. No setbacks occurred. They sailed quickly and easily to Iolcus, entered the harbor, and stepped onto shore. They had succeeded in their quest; they had brought the Golden Fleece to Iolcus.

Afterword

The *Argonautica* by Apollonius of Rhodes ends here, but there is more to the story of Jason and Medea. Hera had wanted Medea to come to Iolcus so that King Pelias would be punished for sacrificing to all of the gods except her. Medea got the revenge that Hera desired. Medea convinced the king's daughters to kill him. She told them that she knew a way to make the king young again, and she demonstrated the process on an old ram. As she said a spell, she killed the ram, cut it up into small pieces, and threw the pieces into a pot to boil. Soon, a young ram jumped out of the pot. Convinced by the demonstration, the daughters of King Pelias killed him, cut his body up into small pieces, and threw the pieces into a pot to boil. But the words that Medea had told them to chant did not have the desired effect. King Pelias stayed dead.

For what happened later, when Jason decided to abandon the sorceress Medea, read Euripides' tragedy *Medea*. Of course, now that you have read this retelling of the *Argonautica*, you should read the real thing.

Appendix A: About the Author

It was a dark and stormy night. Suddenly a cry rang out, and on a hot summer night in 1954, Josephine, wife of Carl Bruce, gave birth to a boy — me. Unfortunately, this young married couple allowed Reuben Saturday, Josephine's brother, to name their first-born. Reuben, aka "The Joker," decided that Bruce was a nice name, so he decided to name me Bruce Bruce. I have gone by my middle name — David — ever since.

Being named Bruce David Bruce hasn't been all bad. Bank tellers remember me very quickly, so I don't often have to show an ID. It can be fun in charades, also. When I was a counselor as a teenager at Camp Echoing Hills in Warsaw, Ohio, a fellow counselor gave the signs for "sounds like" and "two words," then she pointed to a bruise on her leg twice. Bruise Bruise? Oh yeah, Bruce Bruce is the answer!

Uncle Reuben, by the way, gave me a haircut when I was in kindergarten. He cut my hair short and shaved a small bald spot on the back of my head. My mother wouldn't let me go to school until the bald spot grew out again.

Of all my brothers and sisters (six in all), I am the only transplant to Athens, Ohio. I was born in Newark, Ohio, and have lived all around Southeastern Ohio. However, I moved to Athens to go to Ohio University and have never left.

At Ohio U, I never could make up my mind whether to major in English or Philosophy, so I got a bachelor's degree with a double major in both areas, then I added a Master of Arts degree in English and a Master of Arts degree in Philosophy. Yes, I have my MAMA degree.

Currently, and for a long time to come (I eat fruits and veggies), I am spending my retirement writing books such as *Nadia Comaneci: Perfect 10*, *The Funniest People in Dance*, *Homer's* Iliad: *A Retelling in Prose*, and *William Shakespeare's* Othello: *A Retelling in Prose*.

By the way, my sister Brenda Kennedy writes romances such as *A New Beginning* and *Shattered Dreams*.

Appendix B: Some Books by David Bruce

Retellings of a Classic Work of Literature

Arden of Faversham: *A Retelling*

Ben Jonson's The Alchemist: *A Retelling*

Ben Jonson's The Arraignment, or Poetaster: *A Retelling*

Ben Jonson's Bartholomew Fair: *A Retelling*

Ben Jonson's The Case is Altered: *A Retelling*

Ben Jonson's Catiline's Conspiracy: *A Retelling*

Ben Jonson's The Devil is an Ass: *A Retelling*

Ben Jonson's Epicene: *A Retelling*

Ben Jonson's Every Man in His Humor: *A Retelling*

Ben Jonson's Every Man Out of His Humor: *A Retelling*

Ben Jonson's The Fountain of Self-Love, or Cynthia's Revels: *A Retelling*

Ben Jonson's The Magnetic Lady, or Humors Reconciled: *A Retelling*

Ben Jonson's The New Inn, or The Light Heart: *A Retelling*

Ben Jonson's Sejanus' Fall: *A Retelling*

Ben Jonson's The Staple of News: *A Retelling*

Ben Jonson's A Tale of a Tub: *A Retelling*

Ben Jonson's Volpone, or the Fox: *A Retelling*

Christopher Marlowe's Complete Plays: Retellings

Christopher Marlowe's Dido, Queen of Carthage: *A Retelling*

Christopher Marlowe's Doctor Faustus: *Retellings of the 1604 A-Text and of the 1616 B-Text*

Christopher Marlowe's Edward II: *A Retelling*

Christopher Marlowe's The Massacre at Paris: *A Retelling*

Christopher Marlowe's The Rich Jew of Malta: *A Retelling*

Christopher Marlowe's Tamburlaine, Parts 1 and 2: *Retellings*

Dante's Divine Comedy: *A Retelling in Prose*

Dante's Inferno: *A Retelling in Prose*

Dante's Purgatory: *A Retelling in Prose*

Dante's Paradise: *A Retelling in Prose*

The Famous Victories of Henry V: *A Retelling*

Mankind: *A Medieval Morality Play* (A Retelling)

Margaret Cavendish's The Unnatural Tragedy: *A Retelling*

The Merry Devil of Edmonton: *A Retelling*

The Summoning of Everyman: *A Medieval Morality Play* (A Retelling)

Robert Greene's Friar Bacon and Friar Bungay: *A Retelling*

The Taming of a Shrew: *A Retelling*

Tarlton's Jests: A Retelling

Thomas Middleton's A Chaste Maid in Cheapside: *A Retelling*

Thomas Middleton's Women Beware Women: *A Retelling*

Thomas Middleton and Thomas Dekker's The Roaring Girl: *A Retelling*

Thomas Middleton and William Rowley's The Changeling: *A Retelling*

The Trojan War and Its Aftermath: Four Ancient Epic Poems

Virgil's Aeneid: *A Retelling in Prose*

William Shakespeare's 5 Late Romances: Retellings in Prose

William Shakespeare's 10 Histories: Retellings in Prose

William Shakespeare's 11 Tragedies: Retellings in Prose

William Shakespeare's 12 Comedies: Retellings in Prose

William Shakespeare's 38 Plays: Retellings in Prose

William Shakespeare's 1 Henry IV, aka Henry IV, Part 1: *A Retelling in Prose*

William Shakespeare's 2 Henry IV, aka Henry IV, Part 2: *A Retelling in Prose*

William Shakespeare's 1 Henry VI, aka Henry VI, Part 1: *A Retelling in Prose*

William Shakespeare's 2 Henry VI, aka Henry VI, Part 2: *A Retelling in Prose*

William Shakespeare's 3 Henry VI, aka Henry VI, Part 3: *A Retelling in Prose*

William Shakespeare's All's Well that Ends Well: *A Retelling in Prose*

William Shakespeare's Antony and Cleopatra: *A Retelling in Prose*

William Shakespeare's As You Like It: *A Retelling in Prose*

William Shakespeare's The Comedy of Errors: *A Retelling in Prose*

William Shakespeare's Coriolanus: *A Retelling in Prose*

William Shakespeare's Cymbeline: *A Retelling in Prose*

William Shakespeare's Hamlet: *A Retelling in Prose*

William Shakespeare's Henry V: *A Retelling in Prose*

William Shakespeare's Henry VIII: *A Retelling in Prose*

William Shakespeare's Julius Caesar: *A Retelling in Prose*
William Shakespeare's King John: *A Retelling in Prose*
William Shakespeare's King Lear: *A Retelling in Prose*
William Shakespeare's Love's Labor's Lost: *A Retelling in Prose*
William Shakespeare's Macbeth: *A Retelling in Prose*
William Shakespeare's Measure for Measure: *A Retelling in Prose*
William Shakespeare's The Merchant of Venice: *A Retelling in Prose*
William Shakespeare's The Merry Wives of Windsor: *A Retelling in Prose*
William Shakespeare's A Midsummer Night's Dream: *A Retelling in Prose*
William Shakespeare's Much Ado About Nothing: *A Retelling in Prose*
William Shakespeare's Othello: *A Retelling in Prose*
William Shakespeare's Pericles, Prince of Tyre: *A Retelling in Prose*
William Shakespeare's Richard II: *A Retelling in Prose*
William Shakespeare's Richard III: *A Retelling in Prose*
William Shakespeare's Romeo and Juliet: *A Retelling in Prose*
William Shakespeare's The Taming of the Shrew: *A Retelling in Prose*
William Shakespeare's The Tempest: *A Retelling in Prose*
William Shakespeare's Timon of Athens: *A Retelling in Prose*
William Shakespeare's Titus Andronicus: *A Retelling in Prose*
William Shakespeare's Troilus and Cressida: *A Retelling in Prose*
William Shakespeare's Twelfth Night: *A Retelling in Prose*
William Shakespeare's The Two Gentlemen of Verona: *A Retelling in Prose*
William Shakespeare's The Two Noble Kinsmen: *A Retelling in Prose*
William Shakespeare's The Winter's Tale: *A Retelling in Prose*

Anecdote Books

250 Anecdotes About Opera
250 Anecdotes About Religion
250 Anecdotes About Religion: Volume 2
250 Risqué and Controversial Anecdotes
Cool and Funny People: 250 Anecdotes and Stories
The Coolest People in Art: 250 Anecdotes
The Coolest People in Books: 250 Anecdotes
The Coolest People in Comedy: 250 Anecdotes
The Coolest People in the Performing Arts: 250 Anecdotes and Stories
Dance, Music, Theater: 250 Anecdotes and Stories

Don't Fear the Reaper: 250 Anecdotes
The Funniest People in Art: 250 Anecdotes
The Funniest People in Books: 250 Anecdotes
The Funniest People in Books, Volume 2: 250 Anecdotes
The Funniest People in Books, Volume 3: 250 Anecdotes
The Funniest People in Comedy: 250 Anecdotes
The Funniest People in Dance: 250 Anecdotes
The Funniest People in Families: 250 Anecdotes
The Funniest People in Families, Volume 2: 250 Anecdotes
The Funniest People in Families, Volume 3: 250 Anecdotes
The Funniest People in Families, Volume 4: 250 Anecdotes
The Funniest People in Families, Volume 5: 250 Anecdotes
The Funniest People in Families, Volume 6: 250 Anecdotes
The Funniest People in Movies: 250 Anecdotes
The Funniest People in Music: 250 Anecdotes
The Funniest People in Music, Volume 2: 250 Anecdotes
The Funniest People in Music, Volume 3: 250 Anecdotes
The Funniest People in Neighborhoods: 250 Anecdotes
The Funniest People in Relationships: 250 Anecdotes
The Funniest People in Sports: 250 Anecdotes
The Funniest People in Sports, Volume 2: 250 Anecdotes
The Funniest People in Television and Radio: 250 Anecdotes
The Funniest People in Theater: 250 Anecdotes
The Funniest People Who Live Life: 250 Anecdotes
The Funniest People Who Live Life, Volume 2: 250 Anecdotes
History and Politics: 250 Stories
The Kindest People Who Do Good Deeds, Volume 1: 250 Anecdotes
The Kindest People Who Do Good Deeds, Volume 2: 250 Anecdotes
Life is Good: 250 Anecdotes
Maximum Cool: 250 Anecdotes
The Most Interesting People in the Arts: 250 Anecdotes and Stories
The Most Interesting People in Movies: 250 Anecdotes
The Most Interesting People in Politics and History: 250 Anecdotes
The Most Interesting People in Politics and History, Volume 2: 250 Anecdotes
The Most Interesting People in Politics and History, Volume 3: 250 Anecdotes

The Most Interesting People in Religion: 250 Anecdotes
The Most Interesting People in Sports: 250 Anecdotes
The Most Interesting People in Sports (Mostly Baseball): 275 Anecdotes
The Most Interesting People Who Live Life: 250 Anecdotes
The Most Interesting People Who Live Life, Volume 2: 250 Anecdotes
Movies, Radio, and Television: 250 Anecdotes
Resist Psychic Death: 250 Anecdotes
Science and Religion: 250 Anecdotes and Stories
Seize the Day: 250 Anecdotes and Stories

Children's Biography

Nadia Comaneci: Perfect Ten

Philosophy for the Masses

Philosophy for the Masses: Ethics
Philosophy for the Masses: Metaphysics and More
Philosophy for the Masses: Religion

Appendix C: Some Books by Brenda Kennedy (My Sister)

The Forgotten Trilogy
Book One: *Forgetting the Past*
Book Two: *Living for Today*
Book Three: *Seeking the Future*
The Learning to Live Trilogy
Book One: *Learning to Live*
Book Two: *Learning to Trust*
Book Three: *Learning to Love*
The Starting Over Trilogy
Book One: *A New Beginning*
Book Two: *Saving Angel*
Book Three: *Destined to Love*
The Freedom Trilogy
Book One: *Shattered Dreams*
Book Two: *Broken Lives*
Book Three: *Mending Hearts*
The Fighting to Survive Trilogy
Round One: *A Life Worth Fighting*
Round Two: *Against the Odds*
Round Three: *One Last Fight*
The Rose Farm Trilogy
Book One: *Forever Country*
Book Two: *Country Life*
Book Three: *Country Love*
Books in the Seashell Island Stand-alone Series
Book One: *Home on Seashell Island* (Free)
Book Two: *Christmas on Seashell Island*
Book Three: *Living on Seashell Island*
Book Four: *Moving to Seashell Island*
Book Five: *Returning to Seashell Island*

Books in the Pineapple Grove Cozy Murder Mystery Stand-alone Series

Book One: *Murder Behind the Coffeehouse*

Book Two: *Murder in the Library*

Books in the Montgomery Wine Stand-alone Series

Book One: *A Place to Call Home*

Book Two: *In Search of Happiness...* coming soon

Stand-alone books in the "Another Round of Laughter Series" written by Brenda and some of her siblings: Carla Evans, Martha Farmer, Rosa Jones, and David Bruce.

Cupcakes Are Not a Diet Food (Free)

Kids Are Not Always Angels

Aging Is Not for Sissies